"The kisses we sha[...] haunt me..."

Jessie lifted her head, gazing into Hemi's eyes, and felt a clenching deep inside. "Me, too. I can't escape you, Hemi—no matter how hard I try. I run or climb a ravine and I'm still thinking of you. I want you."

"I want you, too. But I'm thinking about what you said—"

She put her fingers over his lips.

"You asked me a question the last time I was here," she said. "I should have just said yes to you then, but fear stopped me." It felt good, finally saying out loud what she'd been trying to ignore for days.

She was afraid to make it too easy for herself to be with him.

Lust.

That was all this was, she reminded herself. That was all she would allow it to be.

They'd be lovers, and when the candidates were done training with her, she'd wave him off and wish him well.

She couldn't help wondering if this was another lie she told herself, but she pulled him to her and took the kiss she craved...

Dear Reader,

I'm really excited for you to read Hemi and Jessie's story. This story combines several passions from my childhood. When I was growing up my parents didn't allow televisions in our rooms, and my mom, fearful that my sisters and I wouldn't have any imagination, closely monitored our viewing time. So most of the shows I watched were with my parents and were educational.

One of our favorite shows was on PBS and featured Jacques Cousteau. My parents were friends with a couple who were marine biologists in Hialeah, where I grew up, and I think I romanticized that profession. I knew I wanted Jessie to be a survivalist but as I was developing her I realized she could have my childhood dream—growing up on a research ship. I loved the contrast of Jessie being so grounded and Hemi always reaching for the stars.

They are both very brash and daring people. I wish I could be the same, but it takes a lot of internal bullying for me to do things that feel risky. In my soul I yearn to try things, but I'm practical, too, and don't want to get hurt :). I once did some cliff diving. But that first leap took me forever!

Jessie and Hemi risk their lives every day just doing their jobs, but the biggest risk of all may be following their hearts.

Happy reading!

Katherine

Katherine Garbera

—

Pushing the Limits

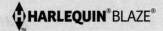

Recycling programs
for this product may
not exist in your area.

ISBN-13: 978-0-373-79952-7

Pushing the Limits

Printed in U.S.A.

USA TODAY bestselling author **Katherine Garbera** is a two-time MAGGIE® Award winner who has written more than seventy books. A Florida native who grew up to travel the globe, Katherine now makes her home in the Midlands of the UK with her husband, two children and a very spoiled miniature dachshund. Visit Katherine on the web at katherinegarbera.com, or catch up with her on Facebook and Twitter.

Books by Katherine Garbera

Harlequin Blaze

One More Kiss
Sizzle

Space Cowboys

No Limits

Holiday Heat

In Too Close
Under the Mistletoe
After Midnight

Harlequin Desire

Baby Business

His Instant Heir
Bound by a Child
For Her Son's Sake

To get the inside scoop on Harlequin Blaze and its talented writers, visit Facebook.com/BlazeAuthors.

All backlist available in ebook format.

Visit the Author Profile page
at Harlequin.com for more titles.

1

JESSIE ODELL STOOD in the corner as the party raged on. The gala for the new Mick Tanner Training Facility was in full swing at the Bar T Ranch just outside of Cole's Hill, Texas. Astronauts, astronaut candidates, government officials and private investors ready to fund missions that would take humanity to Mars all mingled in the converted barn. But she'd had enough of talking about her adventures and the famous people she'd met. That part of her life ended when Alexi slipped into the crevasse on Everest. When she hadn't been able to save him.

She'd known that when she got back to base camp the grief would hit her…except it never had. She'd become icy inside and out. Her old life of making adventure films for television was over—both the thin mountain air and the drive compelling her to move forward. She was tired of having every moment of her life played out for the cameras. She was ready for some privacy.

So this job at the new Cronus mission training center had been a godsend.

"Don't like parties much?" a man asked, coming up on her left to lean against the poorly lit wall.

"Not really," she admitted. He was hard to see clearly in the shadows, just a silhouette of a man in a well-fitting tuxedo. She could tell he was taller than she was—which was saying something, as she was five foot ten and wearing three-inch heels. Her mother had told her to never apologize or cower because of her height and she never had. It was part of her and she couldn't hide it.

"Me either," he said. "I'm Thor, by the way."

"Jessie. Thor, huh? You don't look Nordic."

He laughed and it made her smile, the sound loud and joyful, not low and subtle the way Alexi's had been.

"Yeah. Sorry, it's a force of habit when I'm talking to NASA guys. I guess I should have introduced myself as Hemi. Hemi Barrett. Thor's my call sign and what I answer to. I'm part of the astronaut crew training for the first Cronus mission," he said, stepping from the shadows and holding out his hand.

"You sound American but that name is Maori, right?"

"Yeah. On my mom's side. She and my pops met in Hawaii and I was raised in LA."

His strong jaw and dark stubble accentuated the fullness of his lips. She stared at his mouth for much longer than was acceptable, feeling a spark of instant attraction. She'd never had that before. Normally her sexual desire grew out of friendship with a man.

But this was different. He was different. And this was definitely lust.

His eyes were like melted dark chocolate, decadent

and sinful. His skin was tanned and there were laugh lines around his eyes as well as a one-inch scar on his forehead above his right eye. There was also a birthmark around his right eye. The Maori people called those with these marks *ngā kanohi ora o rātou mā kua wehe atu*, which meant "the living faces of those who have gone on before us." Many believed that the wearer had been marked by the gods for greatness.

He arched one eyebrow at her and she realized she must be staring at him, but she didn't care. She had grown up surrounded by nature. Her first instincts were always driven by the laws of the wild. In the animal kingdom, and in life, she'd found she never regretted not backing down.

She'd spent time with a Maori family on one of her New Zealand adventures. She had also read the personnel files of each of the candidates. But a report couldn't capture the personality of Hemi.

His lips curled in a half smile and he took a step closer. She put her hand out, settling it on his arm, feeling the strength in him under the fabric of his suit jacket. She flexed her fingers. All the men she'd known were lean from surviving in the wilderness. Not him. He was muscled, with coiled strength inside.

His handshake was firm but not meant to intimidate.

"Jessie Odell." He said her name with a hint of awe. That meant he'd seen her show or read her books.

"Yes."

"Wow. I used to watch your parents' show when I was a kid," he said.

Well, thank God for that. She was a part of so

many people's childhoods because of those shows. Her parents—marine biologists—had followed in the footsteps of Jacques Cousteau and had brought her along on their yacht as they filmed their adventures. She'd rather talk about her childhood than her last ascent up Everest. She needed to distance herself from that, which was why she was here in Texas, in a job that would be a cakewalk compared to what she'd done before.

"I bet you hear that a lot," he said.

"Some. Other people want to hear what it was like to snowshoe in the Arctic."

"That's cool," he said with a wink. "But I've been to space."

She laughed and it surprised her. She hadn't expected to laugh tonight, but he was right. She was in a room full of men and women who'd done something extraordinary, as well.

"What's it like?" she asked.

"Buy me a drink and we can exchange stories. I want to hear about the time you were in the shark cage off Africa."

"It's an open bar," she pointed out.

"Then you have nothing to lose," he said.

"Okay, let's go."

They maneuvered through the crowd, where she saw her friend Molly Tanner, owner of the Bar T, dancing with her fiancé, Ace McCoy. Ace would be leading the long-term space mission to build a way station halfway between Earth and Mars.

"Ace has it all," Hemi said, following her gaze.

"Does he?"

"Yeah. He's got a great fiancée, he's first crew

member and leader of the Cronus mission and he's got this training facility up and running."

"Do you want all that?" she asked.

He shrugged. "That's not really a first date kind of question."

"This is a first date?" But she felt a little embarrassed that she'd asked too intimate a question. Usually, when she met people, they were on their way to do something daring, happy to answer intimate questions because there was a risk that not everyone would make it back alive. But he was different. She was curious about him. She'd spent a lot of time working around the world and was usually the outsider. People were used to her asking questions, and at times she forgot herself and followed her own curiosity.

"I'm hoping," he said, with a wink.

That put her at ease a little bit. He had charm, she'd give him that. With his looks and body he probably didn't have to work too hard to get women to fall for him. "We'll see. I still don't know what kind of story you're offering in exchange for hearing about ten-year-old me and a great white."

"The time I did a space walk and became untethered…"

"Obviously you made it back," she said.

"Obviously, but it was pretty dicey for a little while. What's your poison?" he asked as they got to the bar.

Yak butter tea. But she knew that wasn't what he meant. "I'll have whatever you're having."

"Ah, I don't drink," he said. "I have to keep my body in top condition. How do you think I'm doing?"

She let her gaze skim down his body. His shoulders were muscled, his broad chest tapered to a lean waist and long legs. She arched one eyebrow. "You look good, but it could be the cut of your clothes."

He shook his head. "Play your cards right and I might let you see me out of them."

She rolled her eyes at him. It was an over-the-top comment and he knew it. He ordered them each a cranberry juice and sparkling water, and then led the way to a high bar table off the beaten path.

When they got to the table, Hemi handed her one of the highball glasses. Their fingers brushed and a zing went up her arm, leaving goose bumps in its wake.

"To new friends and great adventures."

"To new adventures." She lifted her glass and took a sip.

"New adventures," he repeated. He took a swallow and emptied half his glass.

"Why are you at this party?" he asked. "Are you one of the trainees?"

"No. I prefer to keep my feet on this planet. There are still so many areas I haven't explored," she said, but she knew it was a pat line, no longer true. She'd lost the spirit for adventure. But this man, tonight, awakened her sense of fun and excitement. She wasn't too sure it would last, but fun sounded like a nice change of pace.

"Then what are you doing here?" he asked.

"I'm the survival training instructor. I'm here to make sure all of you spacemen and women know how to survive in any conditions."

INSTRUCTOR.

It explained why someone like Jessie Odell was here. She was well known for her adventures and her television shows. So much excitement percolated amongst the trainees now that Ace had been cleared for preflight, and Dennis Lock, the deputy program manager for the Cronus program, had set their first mission for nine months from now.

"Good to know that they got the best," he said. He had a bit of a fanboy crush on Jessie. She was gorgeous—tall and sexy—and she looked glamorous tonight. Her thick blond hair was pulled up in a twist at the back of her head, with a few tendrils falling to frame her face. Her eyes were the deep blue of the Pacific Ocean around the house he'd grown up in back in California. Her toned arms and long, strong legs were showcased by her silvery dress, and the plunging neckline revealed a hint of the curve of her breasts. "Like what you see?" she asked.

He nodded. "Most definitely. You clean up pretty good. But I think I like you better in a bikini."

"I haven't been in a bikini on screen since I was a teenager."

"I was a teenager, too," he said with a wink.

"Fair enough. So you were going to tell me about almost drifting off into deep space. Is that why you want to be a part of this mission? Did you see something that made you want to keep going?"

She'd put her forearms on the high table and linked her fingers together, and her long diamond earrings swung as she leaned forward. She watched him with those bluer-than-blue eyes and he realized that most people didn't do this. They scanned the room or glanced at their phones. It had been a long time since someone paid such close attention to him.

"I suppose it is part of why I want to go back into space. But I would have wanted that even if I hadn't become untethered."

"How did it happen?"

"Lack of gravity and mechanical failure. The clip on my suit had a small flaw in it and when I lost my balance…it placed too much stress on it and it snapped."

He remembered that moment when he'd felt the snap and started tumbling over, drifting away from the space station. Ace had been wearing a jet-propelled backpack and had come after him, but for about thirty seconds he was free falling into infinity. He'd never been so scared in his entire life, but he'd been cataloging the situation and trying to figure out how to direct his motion back toward the station.

She nodded. "I had a carabiner break one time when I was going up Annapurna in the Himalayas and started sliding down into a ravine. I used my ice pick to stop the descent. But you wouldn't have had anything to grab on to. How did you get back?"

"Ace. He was close by and he came after me. I owe that man my life. Without him…if I'd been up there with anyone else, I'm not sure their reaction would have been as quick."

"It's good to have faith in your crew. There are maybe three people in the world I trust to always have my back in dangerous situations," she said.

"Three? Well, I've got a lot of faith in my crew," he said. "The ones I've been up with, at least. The new candidates I won't know about until we're up there."

"Doesn't that frighten you?" she asked. "That's a bit like relying on luck."

"Don't knock luck. I've seen it serve you well," he said. "That shark attack was incredible. I remember the first time I saw that episode—the network put up a warning at the beginning about its graphic nature. Honestly, I was on the edge of my seat the entire time. What was it like?"

"It was dicey. The truth is, my dad saved me. You probably saw that on TV. The situation was a bit like yours. That cage had been reliable and we'd never had any problems with it, but there was a flaw in the steel that no one could have known about until the structure caved in. The shark lunged, clamped down on the bar and part of my leg…my dad sort of shoved me up to get me out of the way, but the shark got me anyway. Dad punched it hard, on the nose and…"

He put his hand over hers. She seemed fine about the incident. Talked about it the way he might describe falling off his bike when he'd been a kid, but he knew there was more to it than that. It must have been scarier than her tone revealed. "I'm sorry."

"For?"

"Asking about it," he said.

"It's okay. You're not the first. And it's an old memory. Not as fresh as some others."

A fresher near-death experience? He hadn't really followed her career since he'd joined the Air Force to pursue the space program. "Want to tell me about it?"

She shook her head and then took a sip of her drink. "Definitely not."

"Dance?"

"I'm not very good," she said, but put her glass on the table.

"I am," he said, wiggling his eyebrows at her.

"Really?"

"I always tell the truth."

"Always? Really?"

"Yes. Even when I shouldn't," he said. "One of the things my dad drilled into me and my brothers when we were little. My mom is the one who insisted we learn to dance. She said women like to dance and men who won't are missing out."

She smiled. "Sound like good lessons."

"They were," he said.

The band started to play Blake Shelton's "Sangria" and he took her hand, leading her to the dance floor. He pulled her into his arms, leaving a small gap between them. With one hand on her waist and the other holding one of hers, he started to guide her around the dance floor set up in the barn. He soon realized she knew how to dance. Her legs brushed against his and she watched him with the intensity she'd had when they'd been talking.

"Your mom did good," she said.

"She did her best with four rowdy boys."

"Four boys? That must have been some household. Where did you fall in the siblings?"

"Guess," he said. Most people thought he was the firstborn because he had a strong type A personality, but all the Barrett boys did. There wasn't one of them who didn't think he could accomplish whatever he wanted.

"You're confident, but I'm guessing from what

you said about your parents that all the brothers are. You're spoiled, too…so youngest."

"Spoiled? What makes you think that?" he asked.

"You expect to get everything you go after," she said.

"Well…that's just because I'm good. Has nothing to do with being spoiled."

"Yeah, right," she said. "Was I right?"

"You were," he said. "Most peg me for the oldest."

"I can see that, but you don't have that mantle of responsibility. I think if you were the oldest you'd never go to space and leave your family behind."

"Wow. That cuts a little close."

"I always tell the truth, too. Plus, I already know you're a man with his future up in the stars."

"I am. Did you want something else?"

"Like you said, that's a little intense for a first date."

"So this *is* a first date?" he asked with a wink.

"It might be."

"Good."

"Good?"

"Yeah. If there's a first date, that means there'll be more."

"Let's see how this one ends before we go making assumptions," she said.

He liked her.

More than he'd expected from someone he had a fanboy crush on. He'd just seen her in the corner, standing alone, and he'd almost let her stay that way. But there had been something about the quietness of her that had drawn him across the room. Her long, gorgeous legs had helped him make the decision but he hadn't imagined she'd be so real, so genuine, and when she looked up at him with those wide blue eyes, her pretty pink lips parted, she made him think of tangled sheets and long nights spent in each other's arms.

"But I don't think another date is a good idea."

"Why not?"

As the music ended, she said, "Because I'm your instructor, so I think we should keep our relationship strictly professional. Thanks for the dance."

He didn't agree with that. Not at all. There was no reason they couldn't be more than student and teacher. She stepped back as someone called his name. He turned to see who it was, and when he turned back she was gone.

2

JESSIE LET OUT a breath as she entered the gym that had been set up for martial arts training. She was happy that she'd escaped the party and the lights and music. She took her shoes off and let the feel of the mats under her feet ground her.

It was September, and this was just like starting school. When she'd been a kid she'd always wanted to go to real classes, but her parents homeschooled her from their yacht. She was excited about the prospect now.

She'd have preferred to go outside, but she wasn't familiar enough with the terrain at the Bar T. She'd gone on a few hikes to plan survival training exercises for the candidates, but she wasn't ready for a shoeless midnight run.

She left her high heels by the door and crossed to the locker room, where she changed into her white *gi* and fastened her well-worn black belt around her waist. Already she felt like she was breathing more deeply.

She could socialize, but it tired her out. Drained her.

Hemi. Thor. She loved how these astronauts all had call signs. Probably because so many of them had military training. Although Jessie knew that some of this batch of candidates weren't military—weren't even NASA qualified. The missions were a joint effort between NASA and a civilian organization called Final Frontier.

She left the changing room and set her internal timer. She had learned to be very good at monitoring time over the years. She jogged around the perimeter of the gym, keeping her breathing steady and letting her mind drift.

For once her thoughts didn't go to Everest and Alexi. Instead, she pictured Hemi. His face as it was tonight. The smooth confidence of a man who had trained and achieved as much as he had, but also the passion in his eyes. He loved his job. That had been clear.

But she wasn't analyzing him as a trainee right now. She saw, instead, the birthmark under his eye. Thought about the meaning and how Maori folklore suggested he'd been touched by the gods.

She stopped running after fifteen minutes and started going through the different tae kwon do forms that she had learned as a child on her parents' boat, kicking and punching her way through routines that had Korean names like *taegeuk sam jang* and *taegeuk il jang*.

"So this is where you got to."

She finished her forward slicing kick and dropped back into ready position before turning to look at the shadowy doorway. Hemi.

"I can only do parties for so long," she said.

"Me, too." He stepped into the light.

"Really?"

"Yeah. I have to attend a lot of them because of my job but I haven't shut one down in years. You practice tae kwon do?"

She nodded.

"Mind if I join you for a little sparring?" he asked.

Sparring...

"Sure. I'm a third-degree black belt."

"Fourth," he said with a cocky grin. He toed off his dress shoes and tugged at his tie as he walked toward the locker room.

She put her head down, focusing on getting back to her center. Hemi rattled her. She'd come here... who the hell knew why she was in the gym tonight. What she'd thought she wanted to find had eluded her until he'd walked in.

She knew part of her was still grieving. Losing Alexi had been like losing a chunk of her soul. Her parents had said to give herself time. But how much? A part of her would always feel the emptiness of a world without him. But that was her old self. The woman who had found exhilaration in the next new adventure. Her father suspected she'd lost her courage, but her mother feared she'd lost her heart and soul.

Why, then, was she getting that old tingle from being around Hemi? He wasn't doing anything overt...well, he had tracked her down and now he wanted to spar with her.

Was it sex?

Wouldn't it be convenient if this feeling was just lust? Maybe she could have a fling with him. Strictly speaking, it wasn't against the rules, though a part of her did feel like her judgment would be compromised slightly if they slept together. But it might be too late—he was already different from just any student in her mind. He had those big muscly arms and that laugh. She couldn't forget that laugh.

She heard him reenter and he gave her a salute as he started jogging around the gym, loosening up the same way she had.

The last time she'd been alone with a man like this, she'd been with Alexi. The realization hit her hard. He was gone. She wanted to leave.

She turned and was halfway to the door when Hemi caught her wrist and drew her to a stop.

"I didn't peg you as someone who would run," he said.

She wasn't. She never had been. There wasn't a challenge Mother Nature could throw at her that would make her flinch, but this…being one-on-one with a man—a man like Hemi—it was too much tonight.

She was here to rebuild, not to start something… anything…physical with a man—a trainee.

"I'm not running," she said at last, lifting her head to look into those dark brown eyes of his. They were fathomless. He revealed nothing in his gaze. His hold on her was light.

"Is it me?" he asked.

"A little," she admitted. "You are coming on strong, but it's more me. I'm just not sure that this is a good idea."

"Are you sure it's a bad idea?" he asked.

There was something light about Hemi. Something that drew her tired soul, and she knew that she wanted him to convince her to stay. So why the hell was she trying to leave?

"One match," she said. "Then I go."

"I think we should make a wager," he said.

"Do you think you can beat me?" She was known for her skills and for her sheer ability to best any challenge put in front of her.

"Yup. So if I win…you give me that kiss you ran from earlier," he said.

"What kiss? We were dancing," she protested, but she was already assessing him. His strength and size would be her biggest obstacle. Not insurmountable, but still a challenge.

"The one I was planning to steal when the song ended," he said. "What do you want if you win?"

"When I win… I'll leave and you'll stop pursuing me. Deal?"

"Deal," he said, dropping her hand and then moving a few feet away and bowing to her.

"Ready?"

DODGING KICKS AND blocking punches was exactly what he needed. He'd been feeling edgy as he looked around the ballroom earlier. He knew he was one of the top contenders to be named to the inaugural Cronus crew in the next phase, but he also saw the talent there and knew that it wasn't guaranteed. He was going to have to work hard and concentrate.

That didn't mean he couldn't enjoy the ride. His parents had never been much on instant gratification. When someone wanted something, they worked hard, earned it and the family celebrated. It was a lesson that had stood Hemi well all his life.

He didn't pull his punches because he could tell that Jessie wasn't. And it was exactly what he needed. She didn't have strength on her side; physically he had to be at least twice her size, and he worked out constantly to ensure his body was in peak condition. But she was quick and smart.

She had the best reflexes he'd encountered in a sparring partner in a long time.

She clipped him in the jaw with a front snap kick and dropped to ready position as soon as she'd made contact.

"Sorry." She grinned, knowing she'd bested him. "I thought you'd see that one coming."

He rubbed his jaw and shook his head ruefully. "I was distracted."

"By what?"

Her. But that was just hormones…or was it? "I was thinking that I could see why you're so good at surviving."

"You can?"

"Yes. You think fast and are constantly assessing the situation."

She nodded. "That's one of the most important lessons. I'll be talking to your group about that on Monday."

"What could be more important than that?" he asked, watching as she carefully controlled her breathing.

"Not dying," she said.

He laughed.

"It's not funny."

"I know. It's just that Mom used to yell that after us when we'd go off together on our bikes... 'Don't do anything that will get you killed.' We were always doing something...stupid, as Mom said."

"It worked, didn't it?"

"Yeah, I guess it did. It was hit or miss a couple of times."

"Really? I'd have guessed your brothers would always have been trying to keep you safe."

"Sometimes. But I was the baby of our family so they also used to push me. Ace said that's one of the reasons I can take a lot of ribbing from the others on the team. I'm used to it."

And he was. Usually nothing fazed him. He rolled with anything NASA or the trainers or doctors threw at him. But he was feeling...different from his usual attitude. The cosmos still awed him. There was so much out there they simply didn't understand yet. He was a mission specialist with a focus on celestial bodies. Since the beginning of his military career he'd been pursuing a degree in the space-related field of radio spectrometry. His part of the Cronus mission would be to identify the matter that made up the new places they encountered.

"You're looking scary there, Thor."

He shook his head. "Have you ever done anything because it scared you? To prove that you could?"

She gave him a smile that lit up her face. Until that moment he hadn't realized the other ones weren't genuine. This one was.

"Everything I do is for that reason."

He shook his head. "But you seem—"

"Brave, brazen, fearless?"

"Yeah."

"How many times have those same words been applied to you?" she asked.

"Many. They also tend to add in *foolish* and *devastatingly handsome*," he said, because this moment was too heavy. He didn't want to admit to anything real. But he was committed to the truth. Only this time he wanted to dodge it.

She was his trainer; he wanted to seem like the only one who was overqualified for the mission. Not someone who doubted himself.

"I bet they do," she said. "Well, it's time for me to hit the showers. Thanks for sparring with me."

"We aren't done," he said.

"Sadly we are. I beat you, Thor. So this is where I leave you."

She *had* beaten him. "Rematch?"

"Not tonight," she said.

It was then that he noticed the sadness that clung to her. She had hidden it well at the party. In her icy blond looks, most men—himself included—would just see the beauty. Not the woman beneath it.

Maybe it was the *gi* and the fact that she looked tired with her hair falling out of its elegant twist. But he saw that there was something she was running from. Maybe she needed a friend more than a lothario.

"You okay?"

She wrinkled her brow. "Why wouldn't I be?"

He shrugged, then went to the water cooler and filled two paper cones. "You look…"

Sad? He knew he couldn't say that to her. He wasn't dumb when it came to women; he'd watched his parents interact most of his life. They were the strongest couple he knew.

"Like…?" she asked.

"Like you need a friend. Like maybe you want to talk."

She seemed startled by that. And inside he smiled. He didn't want to be predictable, and he realized that he had been until that moment.

"Sorry about earlier. It's just that you're drop-dead gorgeous and for a moment I reacted like a guy and not the gentleman I was raised to be."

She shook her head. "You are smooth, Hemi. I'll give you that."

She called him by his name when she was being real with him. When she wanted distance she used his call sign. Interesting.

"So, want to talk?"

"Not really," she said. "I'm just…"

She took the cone of water from him, downed it and then crumpled the paper in her hands before meeting his gaze again. Her gaze was direct and he thought for a moment that she could see clean into his soul. What did she see in there? He'd been ignoring that part of himself for a while now. Concentrating on working out, doing everything he could to be physically ready for the fight for a spot in Cronus. But he wasn't spiritually ready.

"Can you keep this between us?" she asked.

"Who would I mention it to?" he countered. "I'm not a gossiper."

"I mean…can this just be us, not trainer and trainee?"

He nodded. "I've got your back. Always, Jessie."

She looked over at him. "You surprised me again."

"I did?"

"Yeah. Most people don't think I need someone at my back. They see me on television venturing to extreme places, and think I'm the ultimate loner," she said. "Most don't realize that I have a team climbing with me."

"Honestly, there is something lonely about you, which is how I knew that you needed someone at your back."

JESSIE HAD HER first inkling that this was a bad idea as she followed Hemi out of the gym and down the trail to the lake. He intrigued her. He was big and brash but underneath that muscled exterior beat the heart of a man who knew how to listen. A man who, despite his self-aggrandizing ways, was more than just ego.

She liked him.

That was why this was a bad idea.

The sex thing she could handle. Lust was just a physical reaction to someone. She wanted him, and if they fell into bed together it would be a physical thing. But if she liked him *and* lusted after him…she wasn't ready for that.

The Bar T Ranch consisted of a sprawling house, barns and two bunkhouses. A good five-minute walk away were the new buildings that housed the Cronus candidates and some of the instructors. Candidate housing was in a series of four converted bunkhouses built around a courtyard. Everyone had their own small one-bedroom apartment with a living area and bathroom, and everyone shared a large kitchen. The apartments weren't too bad, but Jessie felt lucky that she'd been given a separate cottage.

All of this did nothing to distract her from Hemi. She should turn around and go to her cottage.

Should.

But she wasn't going to.

It had been a long time since someone new had come into her life and intrigued her the way Hemi had.

"You're awfully quiet," he said.

"Just assessing your trail skills."

Yeah, like he was going to believe that.

"How am I doing?"

"Good," she said. "I noticed you keep to the center of the path, which is good—doesn't leave any trail to be followed."

"Learned that playing hide and seek with my brothers," he said. "The spot I was thinking of is right up here."

They'd both changed out of their *gi* into NASA Cronus mission sweatshirts and exercise pants. And she'd put on a pair of well-worn hiking shoes that she'd stored in her locker a few days earlier. The shoes were very different from the ones purchased new for her Everest climb. The one she'd been on when Alexi's strength had failed him and her skills hadn't been up to the challenge of saving him.

She sighed.

"Here we are," Hemi said, reaching back and holding out his hand to her. "It's a little tricky to navigate in the dark."

She put her hand in his. She'd learned a long time ago to take assistance in new terrain. Though she'd been out here with Ace a few days ago, she still didn't know the land as well as she'd like. But she would. Terrain was her area of expertise. A lot of the training she'd be doing with the astronaut candidates would be in temperature-controlled rooms, but she also had a few excursions planned for them. Surprises that she'd tailor to meet the strengths and weaknesses of the candidates. They needed to be able to react to any situation.

The lake was big enough to supply water for the ranch and the neighboring city of Cole's Hill, and a rough path along the edge joined the main ranch buildings and the Cronus facility. A motion sensor lamp flicked on as they stepped onto the wooden dock that pushed out into the water.

"Here we go," he said, drawing her toward two Adirondack chairs positioned side by side on the dock. She stood there with the breeze on her face and the sound of the water in her ears. She could see the moon's reflection in the ripples as they sat. He smelled of a crisp, expensive aftershave and something masculine, a musk that she was sure was all his own. Something she'd remember long after this job was over and he was gone.

Her father had taught her to classify everything. Touch, scent, sight. She used all of those things to survive.

"The first time I came out here… I was surprised at how noisy it was. I expected it to be quiet—and it is quieter than the city, but not silent."

She smiled over at him. "City boy?"

"Born and bred. I'm at home in the water because I grew up in California, and there isn't a mountain trail

I can't climb, but this...this feels foreign. The cows, the insects. Everything is different here."

"I know what you mean. Most of my childhood was spent on my parents' research yacht or on the island that we called home. I'm good at identifying poisonous insects and avoiding spiky plants that are lethal, but this is different."

He stretched his arm out behind her on the back of her Adirondack chair. He wasn't quite touching her shoulder but she felt his body heat on this cool September evening.

"What scares you, Jessie?"

It was an oddly probing question from someone she'd just met, but considering that she needed to know his fears, she was tempted to answer. Her job for the Cronus missions was to find weaknesses and exploit them to see how far the candidates could be pushed until they broke. And making this about her job made it easier for her. It had been a long ten months since Alexi's death and she wanted to pretend she'd healed, but she hadn't. She knew it by the way she was simultaneously drawn to Hemi and driven to hide from him.

"A situation that I can't control," she said. "I know that control is an illusion but I have techniques for dealing with most of them. Still, there are a few things that elude me."

"Like what?"

"People."

"People?"

"Yes, you can't rely on them," she said. "No one really knows how they will react until they are forced into challenging circumstances. I've been in more extreme places than most and there are still times when I'm not sure what someone will do next."

"Like what?" he asked again.

"Like this," she said, tired of resisting herself and needing to see exactly what Hemi was after. She leaned over and kissed him.

His lips were firm and his breath minty fresh. She felt the dart of his tongue rub over her lips before it pulled back. She tilted her head, deepening the kiss as excitement flowed through her. It had been a long time since she'd experienced this. She felt alive.

She'd been running from him since he'd come up to her at the party. Because he'd immediately made her feel again.

It wasn't deep—hell, how could it be? They'd just met. But it was *something* and she wasn't ready for it. She had to find a moment to breathe.

Breaking the kiss, she took off her shoes before standing up. She looked at him. He watched her silently with those big, dark eyes of his. They were immeasurably deep, like the sea over the Mariana Trench. And that was okay. He wasn't anything to her but a man.

She pulled off her Cronus sweatshirt and pants, leaving her standing in her underwear and bra, before she turned and dove into the lake. The water surrounded her and she found the peace she was never going to find on the land.

3

HEMI WATCHED THE moonlight reflecting first off the lake, then off the woman who was swimming in it. She'd been breathtaking in just her underwear. She was complex, and nothing had helped him understand her better. He had pushed a little too hard because that was his personality. He lived right at the edge, always testing the boundaries to get where he needed to go, and he wasn't about to stop now.

He stripped down to his boxers and jumped into the water after her. It was cold at first, making goose bumps spread over his body. The water was refreshingly brisk, but his body adjusted to it as he swam. Jessie stayed just out of reach, diving under the surface and swimming, finally surfacing and treading water a few feet from him. He trod water next to her for a moment and then shifted to float on his back.

It reminded him of his space walks. How he'd floated there, outside the International Space Station, looking for something in the inky darkness of the cosmos that he couldn't find. Still hadn't found.

He stared up at the constellations, naming them

all in his head, identifying the stars and acknowledging to himself that he still didn't know what it was he reached for. Why he was never close to finding it.

"What's your fear, Hemi? What is it that makes you keep going, after your near miss?" she asked.

He shrugged. He didn't mind asking for her darkest secrets but sharing his own was something else. How could he put into words the emptiness that had been inside him for so long? That would make him seem weak, and he was Thor, mighty, unvanquished, or at least that was how his astronaut brothers and sisters saw him.

"Hemi?" she asked again, her voice hypnotic. As he had always imagined the call of the sirens that led sailors astray.

"I don't know," he admitted. "I keep going up into space and trying to beat records. I train and look for new missions that challenge me and force me to do things others haven't achieved but there is still—" He turned his head and looked over at her. She continued to tread water next to him.

Her long blond hair looked dark plastered against her skull. Some tendrils clung to her bare shoulders, one looping over the strap of her bra. The thin flesh-colored fabric was transparent now that it was wet and he noticed that her nipples were hard. He was trying to be cool and not focus on the fact that she was nearly naked and less than an arm's length away from him.

He struggled to continue their conversation rather than swim closer to pull her into his arms. He wanted to feel their limbs entwined and the warmth of her body against his.

"What?" she asked.

"Something empty inside," he said at last. Damn, he'd meant to keep that to himself, but there it was. The ugly truth he hid from the world—and sometimes from himself. "I don't know what it will take to fill it."

He'd probably have been smarter not to admit this to an instructor who would be evaluating him.

"That's what makes you dare," she said at last, flipping her body to float on her back next to him, her arms spread wide at her sides. "I have the same emptiness inside of me."

"You do?" he asked, his voice deeper and huskier. Somehow, her admission turned him on even more than he already was. She was blunt at times and that honesty of hers was a powerful aphrodisiac. Her hair floated around her head and he couldn't help glancing again at nipples, which were still visible though the cotton of her bra, and looking even harder.

He reached for her, water droplets cascading off his skin, but at the last second he let his arm drop. She was talking to him. Sharing with him as a friend. He couldn't turn this sexual.

But his raging hard-on was making it difficult for him to pay attention to anything other than how she looked.

Maybe she was a siren.

That would explain the spell she had cast over him.

"Everyone does. Most try to ignore it with routines and by filling their lives with stuff, but some people can't ignore it."

"Like whatever made you sad earlier?"

She went still, her hands no longer sculling the water.

"Yes. Like that."

"What was it?"

"My climbing partner and fiancé, Alexi. He wanted things…that even he was afraid to admit."

"Like you? Are you afraid to admit what you want?" Hemi asked. Again, so much easier to turn the spotlight on her.

"Like me," she admitted. "Which is why I'm here trying to teach you and the other candidates all I know about surviving in hostile environments. Maybe that is what I need to finally feel some peace."

"I hope it works for you," he said.

"You do?" she asked.

"Yes. I like you, Jessie. I want you to be happy."

"You barely know me."

"I know, right? But there it is. When you left the party I was like…well, a typical guy and I thought screw it. If Jessie doesn't want me then I don't want her."

She drifted, putting a few feet between them, then cupped her hand on the surface. He had a second to recognize what she was doing before she pushed her hand through the water and a huge splash hit him in the face.

"Screw you, too, Thor," she said, but there was a hint of laughter in her voice.

When he brushed the droplets from his face and looked around for her, she was gone.

The water was still except for the ripples caused by the breeze, and he floated on his back to give his legs a rest. He waited. No matter how at home she felt in the water, sooner or later she'd have to come up for air.

She did—behind him. He heard her surface a second before she once again arched a powerful spray of water at him.

He rolled over and used his water polo experience to do an American crawl toward her. Keeping his head above the surface, he saw the shock in her eyes as he approached. God, he wanted her.

He'd known it earlier.

Hell, he hadn't followed her out of the party and to the gym and then taken her to the lake to cement a friendship. The desire that rocked through him was hot and hard. It made everything else fade away.

He stopped just as their bodies met, put his arm around her waist and used his legs to keep them above the water. Her arms snaked around his neck and her nearly naked breasts pressed against his chest.

His heart beat so loudly he was sure she could hear it, and his blood flowed heavily in his veins.

Her nipples were hard, poking into his chest. He tightened his grip, holding her to him as he looked into her eyes. They weren't lost or lonely right now, and if he had one goal it was to make her forget whatever her pain was.

"You got me, Hemi," she said, rubbing her fingers over his light stubble and then higher, tracing the birthmark around his eye.

She made him proud of the mark, though there were times growing up when he'd wished he didn't have it.

"Do I?" he asked. "I think I might be able to hold

you for this moment, but I'm far from catching you, Jess."

"Jess? I don't believe I gave you permission to call me that," she said.

"Lady, we're nearly naked in a lake together. I'm pretty sure you've given me permission," he said.

"For what?" she asked, her tone challenging.

What was going on in that head of hers? She'd said earlier that she was lonely, admitted to what he had already guessed, but now she didn't seem lonely. It was as if being in the lake had grounded her.

The way that he felt when he was in zero-g, even in the simulator. It made everything clearer when he couldn't control even the simplest things. Was it the same for her?

"Another kiss. That's the only thing I want from you right now," he said. Her lips were full and wet from the lake and the water.

"One more kiss?" she asked. "I doubt that will satisfy either of us."

"Agreed," he said. "But it's a start."

She spread her fingers against the side of his face and ran her hand over his scalp until she held the back of his head. She drew him forward and then scissored her legs to lift herself out of the water. Their lips met and an arch of pure electricity flashed between them.

His cock hardened further and nudged her thighs. His arm around her waist tightened, and for a second, he stopped treading water.

Then he tucked her against his side, lifted his mouth from hers and side-stroked them both to shallower water where he could put his feet down on the muddy bottom of the lake. The water came up to her shoulders.

Safe.

They were as safe as he could make them in this moment. Her strong legs slipped around his and he felt like he'd found something in Jessie that he hadn't been aware he'd been searching for.

It was the last thought he had before he lowered his head, brushing his lips over hers again.

A jolt of adrenaline and lust went through him again and he tangled one hand in her wet hair, pulling her head back so he had a better angle for the kiss. He thrust his tongue into her mouth, feeling her tongue brush over his. Her hand on his head tightened, the other stroked his chest. She squeezed his pectoral muscle before letting her hand drift to his hip. She reached behind him, cupping his butt and drawing him closer to her.

He pulled his head from hers and looked down at her. Her eyes were half-closed, her lips swollen and parted. Her hair drifted out behind her on the surface of the water. And he felt something inside him change.

He couldn't identify it but a part of him knew this kiss was different. Jessie was different. He held her with one arm around her waist and lifted her slightly until her breasts were revealed.

He caught his breath, watching her as she put her hands on his shoulders and then arched in his arms.

Her breasts were thrust upward and forward to him, and he groaned, lowering his head toward one of her nipples. She lifted one hand, pushing it through his wet hair as he licked her nipple and suckled at it through the flimsy bra.

Her legs came up around his waist, and she used her strength to hold herself wrapped around him.

The tip of his erection rubbed against her center and he heard her breath catch. She moaned, and the birds on the shore answered the sound. They were one with each other and the lake.

She slipped her arms around his neck, pulling close so that he couldn't tell where his body ended and hers began. She awakened a hunger in him for so much more than just kisses. But he never wanted to lift his mouth from hers.

He caressed her long back. She had a lean torso with a nipped-in waist. He squeezed her hips and slid his hands lower to cradle her behind. To be honest, her figure was the first thing he'd noticed about her at the party. Her ass was world-class and he'd wanted to cup her cheeks and hold her against his body. And now he could.

His tongue tangled with hers and she sucked on it before leaning back, loosening her arms so she could rest her forehead against his. Her eyes were closed and each of her exhalations brushed over his jaw and neck. She returned her hands to his shoulders as she opened her eyes and he felt her gaze searching his.

It was as if they were made for each other. She was taller than most women and fit him better.

He liked the feeling of her pressed against him. He ran his fingers along the small of her back, saw the gooseflesh spread on her arms and felt her nipples tighten even more against his chest.

She made him forget everything else.

He shifted his hips and rubbed himself against her. The tip of his cock started to slide inside of her. He pulled his hips back before he went any further. *Damn.*

He didn't want to have to think, because she felt so good in his arms, but he lifted his head before the push of lust drove him any further. He was afraid to speak and break the magic of this moment. Of this night.

In that moment he had his answer. He had to talk to her. This woman wasn't his for just one night. They were both on the Bar T Ranch working at the Cronus facility for the next six weeks.

He couldn't screw her and then pretend nothing had happened, because she was different. She made him different.

He put his forehead on hers and closed his eyes, thinking of anything that would cool the lust raging through him. He couldn't just be; he needed to be better.

"Are you on the Pill?" he asked.

He was healthy as a horse and tested often for everything under the sun. He was pretty sure that Jessie was healthy, as well, so at issue for him was the fact that he'd be leaving for a long-term mission in space. He didn't want to leave behind any surprises. Not because he got carried away in the lake with Jessie.

"What?"

"Are you on the Pill?" he asked.

She wedged her arm between them and he let her go. His body was cooling down rapidly now that she was a few feet from him.

"I am. But damn, how did that escalate so quickly?"

she asked. "I'm not... I can't... I... Fuck. I'm sorry, Hemi. I didn't mean for any of this to happen. I'm not really myself."

He nodded.

Be cool.

But he didn't feel cool. He was on fire for her. Obviously her reaction was helping to give him some perspective, but another part of him wondered why something that had felt so damned right to him was making her run away.

She did that a lot, he realized.

She functioned best by retreating when she didn't want to deal with something—or, more specifically, someone.

Him.

"It's okay," he said.

"Thank you," she said. "I know it's not okay and I turned you on and then—"

"We turned each other on, Jessie. I don't know how things got that hot that quickly, but they did. No denying it."

She nibbled on her lower lip and he closed his eyes. Watching her was only keeping him in a state of semi-arousal. He turned and waded toward the dock. He heard her swimming behind him but didn't allow himself to look at her until he'd forced his wet body into the gym pants he'd discarded minutes ago.

He could tell she was behind him, getting dressed, and only when he heard her sit down did he turn to face her. She had retreated inside of herself again and he knew he had to let her go.

She stood up as he reached for his shoes, and their hands bumped. They were so close to each other, he couldn't help himself. He put his hands on her jaw, feeling the wet strands of her hair against the backs. He traced the shell of her ear as he leaned in and kissed her. Not with raging passion but with affection. He kissed her with all the longing in his soul because walking away from her wouldn't be as easy as he knew it should be.

They'd just met, but it didn't feel like that. He wanted to say he knew her but he knew only what she'd let him see—and probably a few things she hadn't meant to reveal.

"I'm sorry things got carried away."

"I'm not. I thought…well, I'm not ready for this, Hemi. I have a class to teach and you're going to be one of my students and…"

"You don't need one of your pupils all hot for teacher. I get it."

She put her hands on his chest and then slid them around his waist, hugging him close and resting her head right over his heart. He struggled to keep his heartbeat from going wild. He didn't want to reveal that holding her made him hot.

"I'm sorry."

She pulled away from him and picked up her shoes, walking up the dock and toward the instructors' cabins. He followed her. His father had drilled it into him that a gentleman always saw a lady home.

He kept his distance, though, because he knew she wanted to be alone.

He'd let her go. He was here for a reason. His sole determination and focus should be on getting onto the crew of the first Cronus mission.

But as she climbed the two steps to the porch of

her cabin and unlocked the door, she glanced back over her shoulder at him. He stood there. Waiting.

There wasn't anything for either of them to say.

He didn't understand, couldn't explain it, but swimming tonight had been the closest thing he'd felt to getting into a rocket and being shot into space.

A woman had made him feel that.

A woman who wanted to keep her distance from him.

"Good night."

"Good night, Hemi."

She went inside and he waited until he saw a light before turning back toward his own quarters. He glanced up at the moon, seeing how it followed him all the way back to his room. He wanted to blame his lack of sleep on the brightness of the moon, but he knew it was Jessie who kept him awake.

4

JESSIE WOKE UP before dawn on her first day of teaching. Her internal clock always got her out of bed at 5 a.m. local time. She made herself a cup of herbal tea and took it out on the deck of her cabin.

She'd trained high-endurance athletes and adventurers who wanted to pit themselves against nature, but this job felt different.

She took a sip of her tea as she settled onto the wooden chair her father had built for her when she turned sixteen. He'd painted it a bright blue, and though time had faded the paint, it was still her favorite chair. She shipped it with her possessions wherever she was currently calling home.

Propping her feet up on the railing, she looked out over the ranch lands. From her vantage point she saw a trail and the tall cedar trees with their twisting roots that were prominent on this section of the land. The trail led to the facility where she would meet her new trainees.

Well, officially.

She'd met most of them at the party last night.

Including Hemi.

His face had haunted her sleep and his questions still drifted through her mind. She wasn't used to being aggressively pursued by a man. It had been a long time since she'd left her rarified life of risk and adventure, and been back here in the so-called real world. Except it had never felt real to her. She'd always floated along, as she had in the water last night, observing. And running away when things got too real.

But after this morning…she wanted to change. She wanted to feel something, though a part of her was very much afraid that she couldn't.

She'd seen breathtaking wonders in the world and done most of the things people put on their extreme bucket lists. And a part of her had lost the wonder that had been her constant companion as a child.

She wanted it back.

But she had no idea how to reclaim it.

For a moment last night, when she'd been in the lake with Hemi beside her, she'd had a glimpse of what could be.

She took another sip of her tea, tipped her chair back on its rear legs and looked up at the roof of her wooden porch. Spiderwebs and some scratch marks. She put the chair down on all four legs and stood on the seat, reaching up to touch the scratches. Initials.

WBT.

No doubt one of the co-owners' relations. The Tanners' forebears had been granted this land by the Spanish king back before Texas was a state. She wondered what those people must have felt, looking out at this land, trying to figure out how to claim it.

She heard the rhythmic sound of footsteps approaching on the trail and climbed down off the chair as a group of six Cronus candidates came jogging around the bend.

Hemi was in the lead, followed closely by two women, and then a man and two more women.

They waved at her as they continued running by. She watched them go and realized that she'd never been a part of a team. Her family had been a group of individuals and most of the adventures she went on pitted her against nature. There were other people on the same quest but she'd always been aware that she was the leader, and the responsibility she had for their safety had been heavy.

The Cronus candidates were a team. She heard them urging one another on. There were twenty-four candidates out here competing for places on the missions. And everyone wanted to be part of the first one.

She'd read the files of each of the candidates and understood that each of them was elite in some way. They also had a fire to be up there among the stars. She finished her tea and went back inside, doing a series of tai chi exercises that helped bring her peace. Then she showered, tossed her hair into a ponytail and put on khaki cargo pants and a black T-shirt.

The exercises she had designed for her students were tough. But her mandate from Dennis Lock had been to get these people ready for anything. To hone their instincts so that they would be able to survive anything that nature or failing technology put in their way. He had said that ensuring no one died in space was mission critical. She understood that.

So today she'd teach them things that she'd learned
from the time she was old enough to walk. Ways of
moving into a new area and assessing the potential
threats, and then she'd test them. She had a mock
ship interior that she'd be using along with the tech-
nical crew. Her part of the training involved using
the mock ship interior and working with the crew
candidates. She knew that they were going to assess
the dynamics between the contenders to ensure that
the first mission was a success.

She had spent a lot of time in their space suits
and in the mock module herself, trying to make sure
she understood what was going on. She had to teach
them how to survive if their climate control was
damaged and the icy cold of space permeated their
ship. Though their astronaut training had already
covered this, she was here to shore up their under-
standing of how to survive when everything went
wrong.

She knew that all she could do was give them the
tools they'd need to survive and she was determined
they would.

Last night had been fun, she thought, as she applied sunscreen and lip balm. A sort of sweet dream.
An anomaly. Today it was back to her world—teaching
people to survive. Hemi, with his brash attitude, flashed
into her mind and she felt a flicker of excitement. That
was different—the first time in a long time that a person and not a challenge had inspired it.

Interesting. And scary. She was going to have to
step away from Hemi but she had more than a few
regrets at the thought.

HEMI HAD DONE his best to play it cool when he'd jogged past Jessie's cabin that morning. But he wasn't cool. Granted, a big part of his attraction to her was down to the fact that she was hard to get, although he knew she wasn't playing. That wasn't her way.

She was honest and tall and so damned beautiful he'd spent more than half the night in a semi-aroused dream state, wishing last night in the lake had ended with them together in his bed.

The memory of her full breasts pressing against the almost transparent fabric of her wet bra, her eyes bright, blond hair a halo in the light of the waning moon, was burned into his mind. It was all he saw when he closed his eyes, and the effect on him was definite, immediate and pronounced. Even running and pushing himself to his limits, his body had reacted to the thought of her. He had been in lust before. Hell, who hadn't? But this was different. And he didn't need lust messing up his focus.

He'd worked so hard to get where he was. He didn't want to lose his chance to be second-in-command on the first Cronus mission because of the power of the boner. He needed to get his head back into the game.

One cold shower later he felt more in control. He leaned over the sink in his bathroom and stared at himself in the mirror. He looked at his face and tried to remind himself of everything that was important. Everything he wanted and needed to be happy in his life.

He touched the birthmark that bordered his right eye. His mother had called it his good luck charm, and this morning he'd take luck. Though he had earned everything he'd achieved, every once in a while he'd take his mom's belief that his ancestors had marked him for greatness.

He rubbed his hand over his jaw, deciding he didn't need a shave, and then got dressed for the day. They had a schedule that was packed with lessons and training. The Cronus team would be using a spacecraft that had been designed for the lengthy mission and they all had to learn how to repair it. They'd be traveling a long way before assembling the way station.

The way station was halfway between Earth and Mars. Each mission would add to the station, but initially it would be just minimal living quarters to support a five-man crew. The mission would last twenty months. Eighteen months would be spent just traveling to and from the station. They were tentatively scheduled for two months to assemble the station and live on it before returning to Earth.

Of course, he also had an extreme survival class in the afternoon with Jessie. Hopefully he'd be focused on the course and not the instructor. He needed to be. He'd seen how close his good friend Ace had come to being dismissed from the Cronus team because of his health, and had almost been moved into an administrative role. Dennis wasn't taking any chances with this. They all had to be in top shape.

And that meant not lusting after a tall, cool blonde.

Shaking his head, he headed out of his quarters. The apartments weren't too bad and Ace had recommended that all of them bring stuff that reminded them of home.

Hemi hadn't brought much. His home was up there in the stars, so he had tacked up a poster of the area where Cronus would deploy the way station. Then he'd hung a list of his own objectives on the wall at the foot of his bed so he would see them every morning.

He ducked into the kitchen and grabbed a protein smoothie from the fridge. Walking down the hallway, he found Izzy Wolston locking her door. Her call sign was Bombshell, but behind her back some of the guys called her Ice Queen. She was a little cold at times, but she was built like a pinup girl, with a curvy body and heart-shaped face. A lot of men, himself included, sometimes got distracted by the curves and missed the keen intelligence in her eyes.

"Ready for this?" she asked.

"Yeah. I've been ready since we got here. The party last night felt like one big tease," he said.

She nodded. "I heard the higher-ups wanted to give us a chance to acclimate before we got started training."

"More like they were sizing us up," Hemi said.

"Agreed. I think we've been under observation since our names were announced," she admitted.

"Probably."

They walked over to the training facility in silence, past the lap pool and chin-up bar in the open courtyard.

They entered the main auditorium, which would be used for all general sessions. Everyone had been given a schedule for training and it was vigorous. Hemi glanced over his, making sure he'd been given dedicated time in the observation room to analyze data being sent back by the explorer satellite from the region where they would build the way station. Part of

Hemi's role was to ensure that there were no anomalies that would interfere with the safety of the station.

The scent of fresh mountain flowers drifted on the air and a second later he spotted Jessie standing a few feet away talking with Ace and one of the nutritionists. He watched her for a long moment before forcing himself to turn away.

Down, boy, he thought, but the truth was that he really struggled not to go over there and make small talk, just to hear her voice again.

She'd gotten under his skin.

A part of him thought it had happened too quickly, but his father had fallen for his mom in a second. That was what his dad always said, that he'd seen her at a Pacific Culture Festival doing a reading of Maori *mana wahine* poetry. Her voice had been compelling and his father had been drawn to her. She had exuded confidence and power, and his father said he'd known she would be important to his life.

It had sounded like bullshit to Hemi. He didn't doubt his father loved his mother, but that any woman could floor a man before he even spoke to her had sounded…well, like a tall tale. But then he'd seen Jessie last night.

At first he'd thought maybe it was because she'd been his crush as a teenager, but then, as they'd talked, the crush had disappeared and it had become about Jessie.

Jessie.

He heard her laugh and turned toward her again, took a step in her direction before he realized what he was doing. He turned on his heel, leaving the auditorium to get control of himself.

"WELCOME TO SURVIVAL TRAINING 101. I've read your files and seen the training you've already had, so I know some of you have learned some of this already. But I promise that is just the beginning." Standing in a classroom in front of twenty-four candidates wasn't Jessie's ideal situation.

She felt claustrophobic, the back of her neck itchy in the nearly windowless room. Most of the facility was fortified with heavy walls. The work took place in simulators and specially designed modules. The Cronus trainees also practiced teamwork through practical ranching sessions. Jessie had seen the setup in the barn—Ace had the teams take turns every day riding the roundup, driving cattle from one pasture to another.

She glanced through the one small, heavily tinted window, trying to see the sun, and decided to put up some posters of outdoor scenes. It was the only way she'd tolerate being inside for any amount of time.

"Because of the nature of what I'm teaching you to react to, there will be times when you will be...well, *surprised* is the best word I can think of. And you'll be forced to react to a situation," Jessie said. "I can't tell you when that will happen, but over the next six weeks there will be a number of unexpected activities that will test a myriad of skills. Some of them will be the ones I've taught you but they will also include standards from some of your other classes, as well."

"Let the fun begin," Hemi said, and the candidates in the room grinned.

"Don't know about the rest of you, but I'm ready for something to happen," another candidate chimed in. From her files, Jessie knew she was Isabelle Wolsten, call sign "Bombshell."

There were mumbles of agreement.

"Great. We are going to start with extreme cold. In case you aren't familiar with me, I've been on several climbing expeditions to Everest and the other nine highest peaks. Today our topic is what to do when the unexpected happens. NASA has already provided you with the training for what to do in the capsule and on your ship, but what happens when something goes wrong? How will you survive when the temperature drops unexpectedly and you are trapped without the tools you thought you had?"

Many of the candidates pulled out their notebooks and laptops and started writing. She started with the basics; for example, how staying warm was easier than getting warm again once hypothermia started to set in. She talked about how she stayed warm in the wilderness, using a lifetime of knowledge that was second nature to her. She didn't have to think about what she would say next, so she let her eyes drift over the candidates. This was a pretty even mix of men and women. There were a few accents in the group, and Hemi was by far the largest man, but they all looked very fit. She'd learned since being at the Cronus facility that healthy muscle mass was important to reducing the health risks associated with being in space.

"Let's take a break. There are protein shakes in the other room and I'll join you in a few moments," Jessie said.

Most of the candidates filed out, but Hemi lingered and she walked over to him. He smelled good.

His aftershave was…woodsy, spicy, addictive, she thought. Last night had been…a mistake. She knew it. She wasn't here to have a fling with a candidate or even to become buddies with anyone. She was here to teach.

"What's up?" she asked. She really needed Hemi to follow the others, since they were going to be exposed to extreme cold in less than five minutes.

"I know we said—"

"I can't do this right now," she interrupted. "Can we talk later? Maybe tonight after dinner?"

"I have to log time in the observatory," he said.

"Can I meet you there?" she asked, trying to usher him toward the door.

"Sure," he said. "But this won't take long."

She nodded and realized he wasn't going to budge until he was good and ready.

"Okay."

"I felt a connection with you last night, Jess. I know you said that we have to work together and we'd be better off keeping our distance, and normally I'd agree, but my mind and my body aren't getting the same message."

She closed her eyes. Her body hadn't exactly wanted to get that message, either. But she knew that it would be a mistake for her to get personally involved with him. Everything about him, including the sexual attraction that had made it difficult to sleep last night, was like a big glaring sign to turn back. To go to her safe place and wait for the storm to pass.

"Let's talk about this later," she said again, glancing at the clock and realizing that she now had two minutes to get him into the break room with the other candidates.

"Really talk, or is this just another delaying tactic?" he asked.

"Truly, it's a little bit of a delay. I'm teaching and I've never done it with this big a group before, or where the stakes are so high. That's partially why I wanted to slow things down between us. Also, I really need some water," she said. "I don't usually talk that long."

He nodded. "Let's go. I guess I'll see you at the observatory tonight."

"Great. Thank you, Hemi."

She followed him out of the room and down the hall into the break room. She scanned the candidates, counting to make sure they were all present. There was one remaining health shake on the table, and Hemi went and grabbed it.

"Want a sip of my drink? There might be some water bottles in the fridge," he said.

"I'm good. I have a water bottle in my locker. I'll be right back," she said, stepping out and pushing one of the buttons on the door to lock it and start dropping the temperature.

Through the window in the locked door she made eye contact with Hemi. He arched one eyebrow at her and downed his shake. He knew that this was a test, she realized. She turned to go to the observation room.

She'd done her job and now she wanted to see if Hemi was as good as she thought he was—he and all the other candidates. As the test progressed and she, Ace McCoy, Dennis Lock and Dr. Tomlin watched her students, she felt a sense of pride in Hemi. He was a natural leader and he remembered a lot of the things she'd discussed in class.

When the simulation ended, she hit the button to start the return to normal temperature in the room. "Good job, everyone. You are all quick studies."

"Indeed," Ace said. "Report to the gym and your assigned treadmill. We want to see how the cold affected your reflexes. I'll be leading the crew training in the simulator. Dr. Tomlin and her team also want your vitals."

Jessie knew her part in the exercise was over, so she stayed in her chair making notes and pretending she wasn't sneaking glances at the live footage of Hemi as he ran on the treadmill.

Which was proving harder than she'd like.

5

"THE TESTS WENT pretty well," Dennis said as Jessie sat down in his office. As deputy program manager for the Cronus program, he had other responsibilities that required him to be at the Johnson Space Center, as well. He alternated weeks between Cole's Hill and Houston.

"I thought so. I think it was a nice emergency test and I'd love to see the results after they've had more training. A few candidates seemed totally nonplussed by the exercise," Jessie said. She pulled her notebook closer to her and looked at the names she'd jotted down. It had been obvious that Hemi was at the top of his class.

"Me, too. Ace and Dr. Tomlin are meeting with me weekly to assess the candidates. I'd like you to start sitting in on those meetings, as well. They are Fridays at ten. On the weeks I'm in Houston we'll use the video conference."

"Sounds good," she said, jotting a note in the top corner of the notebook. She wasn't used to meetings and classes but had been adjusting pretty well to them.

One thing she realized about working for NASA—there wasn't a lot of time to dwell on the past or what might have been.

She had to stay very grounded in what was going on now. But ignoring her attraction to Hemi wasn't the smartest decision.

"That's all for now. We'll review how the candidates are responding to your lessons every week. Then you might need to adjust what skills you're focusing on."

"I'm happy to do that," she said, gathering her stuff and getting ready to leave. She looked over at Dennis. His eyes were dark with shadows and there were lines around them. Laugh lines or stress? She didn't know him well enough to speculate.

If today had shown her one thing it was that she wasn't going to be able to just walk away from Hemi. She couldn't ignore him. She was interested in him.

"One more thing," she said.

"Yes?"

"I… There is…one of the candidates and I…I know there's not a direct antifraternization policy here but if a trainer and trainee were dating, would that be okay?" Damn. That was very awkward and not at all what she'd been expecting to come out of her mouth. But she wanted to be sure she wasn't putting Hemi's chance at getting on the first mission in jeopardy by meeting him later tonight.

Dennis leaned back in his chair, stretching his arms over his head. "No. There is no policy. But I think that if any of the candidates is distracted it might hurt their focus. Also, as a trainer, how objective can you be when it comes to assessment?"

"I agree. I'm not pursuing anyone," she said, and then realized she sounded like she was a defending herself.

"I didn't think you were. Human nature is damned interesting," Dennis said. "Met my wife at a meeting at the Pentagon more than twenty years ago. She was not amused that I couldn't keep my eyes off her legs… but the woman has really nice legs. Whatever happens, you're all adults and unless it causes a problem, I think you are fine."

She gave him a small smile. Human nature was interesting. Why was Hemi so fascinating? And why had she met him now? She had to make very sure that she didn't lose her objectivity where he was concerned.

"Thanks, Dennis."

"No problem. See you next week," he said.

She let herself out of his office and went to the gym, but the treadmills were all occupied and she really didn't want company. She left the facility and went back to her cabin, where she found a note taped to her front door.

Jessie,
I have to do a night training exercise with the team. Would you be available to talk tomorrow morning? I run at 6 a.m. if you want to join me.
H

She felt simultaneously relieved and let down. She was glad that she didn't have to talk to him tonight. This would give her more time to find her sense of normalcy, instead of the out-of-control way he made her feel.

But at the same time she was keenly disappointed she wouldn't see him. Which was a warning in itself. She walked through her cabin, flicking on the ceiling fans as she went and stripping out of her clothes. The uniform that all of the instructors wore was a collared royal blue shirt emblazoned with a NASA logo and a pair of black cotton trousers. The clothes were comfortable, but she wasn't.

She had been inside too much today.

Maybe that was what was really behind her feelings of disappointment. She opened her dresser and grabbed the first T-shirt she touched. She pulled on a pair of jogging shorts and bent down to find her all-terrain trail shoes, then slipped out the back door. She had on sunglasses and her hair was in a high ponytail.

As she started jogging she was aware of her surroundings, but slowly everything fell away as she ran.

Gradually she felt more like herself. This was what she needed. She kept on moving until she reached the ravine Molly had mentioned. It was deep and had been formed by the flash floods that occurred during the rainy seasons.

Slowly and carefully she made her way down the path to the bottom. A trickle of water and some damp sand were all that remained of the river. She stood there at the bottom, looking forward to the challenge of scaling the side of the ravine and climbing out.

This she could handle. Give her an obstacle, and she could analyze it, figure it out, conquer it.

Not like most people. Not like Hemi.

She could handle it, though. One of the things

she'd always been comfortable with was putting men in boxes, separating them from the rest of her life. Dennis had been right about human nature, but she knew her own and she always came out on top.

HEMI LEFT HIS quarters after midnight. He was tired from a long day of lessons, tests and training, but he couldn't sleep. He had no destination in mind and was surprised to find himself at the lake.

He really shouldn't have been surprised considering he'd spent most of his waking moments thinking about Jessie and this very spot.

Regret wasn't something he wore well. He was decisive and always went after what he wanted…or so he'd believed until he met her.

She confused him.

It had been three days since her first class and the extreme cold test and though he'd invited her to join him on his morning run, she hadn't shown up.

His brother Manu had told him a long time ago that the only thing a man got from running after a woman was winded.

The advice lingered in the back of his mind as he walked to the edge of the dock. He sat down on the edge, took off his shoes and socks and dangled his feet in the water.

The night was calm and quiet. A breeze rippled through the trees that surrounded the lake, as birds and crickets made their soft cries.

He should feel peaceful but he was edgy.

He heard footsteps on the dock but didn't glance around. He wanted privacy. He'd come out here to be alone. Or so he thought until he caught the scent of her body spray on the wind.

Jessie.

"Didn't expect to see you here," she said.

He shook his head. "I know."

"You know?"

"You've been avoiding me, Jessie. Doesn't take a genius to figure out you wouldn't be here if you knew I was."

"I'm not avoiding you," she said, kicking off her shoes and sitting down next to him.

"What do you call it then?"

"Being smart," she said at last. She put her hands behind her hips and leaned back on her elbows, swinging her legs in the water and making droplets cascade from her feet.

"Smart?"

"Yes," she said. "I'm lost. There, I said it. I sort of alluded to it the other night, but the truth is I've been lost for a while now and I'm not sure who I am anymore. That's the worst possible time to get involved with a man. Especially a man like you."

He turned his head. Processed the fact that she had contemplated getting involved with him. Maybe he still had a shot at changing her mind.

"What do you mean, a man like me?" he asked. His own voice sounded too loud in the quiet of the night.

She sighed. "You are so confident, so sure of who you are, that it would be easy for me to fall into something with you, and then I'd start to see myself as you saw me…maybe even believe that I was the woman you saw, but it would be a lie."

Her honesty cut through the bullshit he'd had ready. Lines he'd used in the past that he was 90 percent sure he could have used again on her if she hadn't been so damned honest.

"It's not helping," he said at last. "I get what you're saying and I'm not that sure I would do that. I see a woman who is strong and brave and who dares do things that I would never try. That is part of who you are, Jess."

She looked over at him, her long blond hair sliding over her shoulder. "You think so? I don't. Those are the very characteristics that were drummed into me as a child."

He pulled his feet from the water and turned to her, smiling. She sat up and faced him.

"That is the core of who you are. What is it you feel you've lost?" he asked.

"My soul," she said, then tipped her head back to look up at the sky. "I can't feel things like I used to. It's as if the day Alexi slipped into the crevasse some part of me went with him."

He didn't know what to say to help her see that she was still grieving for Alexi. That she maybe thought there was something she could have done differently. He wasn't sure, but he figured time was the only cure.

And maybe a new lover…

But that was his body talking. Since she'd sat down next to him all he could think about was her mouth and what it had been like to kiss her. She'd tasted good and her mouth fit under his perfectly. He felt no shame in admitting that when she talked in class all he did was watch her lips, remembering how they'd felt against his.

"His death is going to take time to come to terms with," Hemi finally said.

She didn't respond, but after a minute she scooted closer to him and put her head on his shoulder. He knew she needed a friend and he hoped he could be one to her. But that didn't mean they weren't attracted to each other. She might be living in the past and thinking of her future, trying to figure out where she would go from here, but he was living in the present, wanting more than anything to tip her head back and take the kiss he craved.

"Tell me something about the stars. Do astronauts have tales like sailors do?" she asked. "Distract me, Hemi."

Distract her. He needed to distract himself. "Have you ever heard the story of Vega?" he asked. It was one of the night stars that was most visible and part of the Summer Triangle.

"I've heard of Vega. What is the story?"

He put his arm around her shoulder and shared the Japanese tale that his father had heard growing up in Hawaii. His parents had met and married in Hawaii, but had moved when his father was offered a teaching job at UCLA.

"The Japanese celebrate the *tanabata* festival on the seventh day of the seventh lunar month. The festival is about the story of Princess Orihime, the daughter of the *tentei*, or 'sky king.' She was a renowned weaver, but because she worked so much, she was lonely. Her father was worried about her, so he arranged for her to meet Hikoboshi, the cowherd, and the two immediately fell in love and married. But they were so wrapped up in each other, they neglected their work. Orihime's father was angry that she'd stopped her beautiful weaving, so he separated the lovers, putting one on one side of the Celestial River—or Milky Way—and one on the other. They're represented by the stars Vega and Altair. They can see each other but never meet."

"That's so sad," she said.

"Yes, but on the seventh night of the seventh moon, a bridge of magpies forms across the Celestial River, and the two lovers are reunited," he said. "But if it rains, the magpies can't form the bridge. So the Japanese always hope for clear skies on Tanabata."

"That's such a beautiful, sad story. Thank you, Hemi," she said, tipping her head back.

He wanted to blame it on the moon but knew it was his own lack of self-control and desire for Jessie. He leaned forward and brushed his lips over hers, claiming the kiss he'd been craving for an eternity. He felt like he was a cowherd around her and that she was the celestial princess. Someone he could only glimpse and never hold.

No matter that she thought her soul was lost; he knew that he would be the one to get lost in her. Because she called to him like only the cosmos had before.

DAYS OF PRETENDING that she'd made the right choice when she'd ignored his invitation were finally over.

His mouth was full and firm, and he kissed like he did everything—boldly. He put his hand on the nape of her neck and stroked her exposed flesh, his finger moving up and down until she turned more fully into him and put her arms around his chest, drawing him to her.

She pulled her head back from his and looked into those big, dark brown eyes. She read the passion and desire there, but also saw that it was controlled. He was ready for her to say no. To put the brakes on. And he still kissed her with an open honesty that made her want him all the more.

She put her forehead on his shoulder, hiding from the truth.

This attraction wasn't going to go away.

"I can't sleep without thinking of you in my arms. The kisses we shared here in the lake haunt me," he said, his voice was almost guttural.

She lifted her head and, gazing into his eyes, felt a clenching deep inside of her. "I can't, either. I can't escape you, Hemi, no matter how hard I try. I run or climb a ravine and I'm still thinking of you. I want you."

"I want you, too. But I'm thinking about what you said—"

She put her fingers over his lips to stop him from talking. She didn't want to think anymore. She'd been debating for days about what she should do. How she wasn't in a position to get involved with anyone. But in the end she was here in his arms and what she felt right now wasn't regret.

"You asked me a question the last time I was here," she said.

"I did?"

"Yes. You asked me if I was on the Pill, and I am. I should have just said yes to you then, but fear stopped me," she admitted, finally saying out loud what she'd been trying to ignore for days. She was afraid to make it too easy for herself to be with him. The man who was so sure of himself, who wanted to do dangerous things that she couldn't save him from. The man she couldn't stop thinking about.

Lust.

That was all this was. That was all she would allow it to be. She wanted him. They'd be lovers, and when the candidates were done training with her, she'd wave him off and wish him well.

She stood up and he pushed himself easily to his feet. He stopped to gather their shoes, handing hers to her. Then they joined hands and walked slowly up the path.

She liked the feeling of her hand in his, and when they got to the fork in the trail she tugged him up the path that led to her cabin. She tossed her shoes on the porch, then drew Hemi through her front door.

"Come here, woman," he said.

She smiled at him and shook her head. It would be too simple to get lost in him. That hadn't changed. She wasn't going to give over control that easily. She crooked her finger at him and beckoned him to her as she leaned against the door.

"You come here," she said.

And he gave her a grin that made every feminine instinct she had spring to life and her blood flow heavier in her veins. He walked toward her like a tiger stalking its prey, and when he was close, she pulled him to her and claimed the kiss she'd craved. Not the bold, testing one he'd taken at the lake, but one that wouldn't end until they were both naked and wrapped in each other's arms.

6

THE HARDWOOD UNDER his bare feet was cool and soothing after the trail they'd walked up. His jeans felt too tight and his T-shirt constricting. She stood there, the adventurer he knew her to be. Someone who was willing to take what she wanted, and nothing turned him on more.

She had said she was lost, but she didn't look it.

He stopped when there was only an inch of space between them. Her hair fell in soft waves around her shoulders and he reached out, capturing one curl with his hand. He wrapped it around his finger and she tipped her head to the side, studying him carefully as he did.

"You're sure about this?" he asked.

She nodded, the motion tugging his hand. He let the curl fall and placed his open palm on her collarbone. He only had to bend the slightest bit to kiss her. He liked that. She was tall and strong and beautiful. He wanted to help her find herself again.

Not because of the mission, but because she was Jessie and she was different to him.

He pushed that aside. He wanted to feel, not think. To see her naked and then caress every inch of that elegant body of hers.

He moved his hand until he held the side of her neck and stretched his thumb to rub it over her lips. They parted and she sucked his thumb into her mouth.

He felt a jolt in his groin as he hardened. His clothes, which had already felt restricting, were now way too tight. He reached down with his free hand and undid his fly to give his cock some space.

She reached between them, her hand running slowly down his chest before sliding her hand inside his jeans. Every touch of her hands on him caused a fire to spread in his soul. She reached down to cup his balls, squeezing gently. His hips jerked forward, and he pulled his thumb from her mouth and rubbed the wetness on her mouth before leaning forward to take her bottom lip between his teeth.

She threw her head back and arched her spine, and he wrapped his free arm around her waist, supporting her while he thrust his tongue deeper into her mouth.

Damn.

She tasted as good as he remembered and he was so hungry for her. No matter how deep the kiss was, it still felt like it wasn't enough. Her hand moved on his balls and he felt that shiver down his spine that meant he was close to coming. He canted his hips back from her and felt the tips of her fingers on his shaft. She lightly brushed them up and down, teasing him to within an inch of his orgasm.

He grabbed her wrist and pulled her hand from his cock. He lifted her off her feet and walked the two steps it took to get to the sturdy wooden console table against the wall. He set her down on it and stepped between her legs, skimming his hands up and down her waist, slipping one hand under her T-shirt.

Her skin was soft to the touch and he felt a little tremor go through her as he pushed the fabric of her shirt higher, revealing her midriff, which was flat and tan. He wrapped his hands around her sides, felt her ribs underneath his fingers as she breathed, the weight of her breasts brushing against his hand, and he couldn't help snaking one finger up and grazing her nipple through the fabric of her bra. She shivered and arched in his hands, and then pulled her T-shirt off, tossing it aside.

He shifted back to look at her. Her shoulders were squared, causing her back to arch, and her hair was in disarray. A blush started in the middle of her chest and spread up her neck. Her sports bra was plain cotton, doing its job without frills. The kind she'd use in the wilderness, that would dry quickly. It suited her.

She was so much a part of the earth, he realized. Strong, nurturing—all the things that the planet was. And he wanted to be grounded with her. He needed that grounding, something solid to hold on to while his future called him away. But now they were together.

Her breasts were larger than he had realized, contrasting with her small waist. Her shorts rode low on her slim hips and he caught his breath as she slid her finger slowly under the waistband.

"Your turn to take your shirt off," she said.

A shiver went down his spine. He liked that she was taking control. Her strength matched his in every way. "I'm not done looking at you yet."

She tipped her head to the side. "Like what you see?"

"Very much." She really was like a siren, and she drew him like no other woman ever had.

He spread his fingers out and ran one hand over her stomach, down to her belly button. It was a flat, tiny indentation on her body and he skimmed his finger around it, then moved lower, pushed his hand underneath her shorts and ran his fingers along the lines of her hip bone. Then he wrapped his other arm around her and lifted her off the console.

He pushed her shorts down to her knees before setting her back down.

She moved her legs back and forth until her shorts slid down to the floor. Her sporty bikini underwear matched her bra. As he looked at her, she put her hands on the table and leaned backward.

She was all confident, sexy woman, and he responded to her as if she were the only female on the planet. She was for him. She was his.

She wrapped her legs around his hips and drew him forward with a tug on the hem of his shirt. He leaned over her, putting his hands on the wall behind her head, and felt the warmth of her breath against his chest. The wall was cold compared to the heat she awoke in him.

She pushed his shirt up his body, her fingertips brushing over the Maori tattoo on his side. He shivered as she traced over it. Something primal stirred deep inside of him.

"Is this something you liked or is it significant to your family?" she asked, leaning forward. He felt her breath against his side as her fingers traced the swirling design of the tattoo.

"Family," he said. "My ancestors were from New Zealand and this was originally a facial tattoo."

He took her hand, brought it to the swirl that curved down toward his hip bone and then ended in a point. "It tells of my family's history and which tribe we belonged to. Sadly that meaning was lost. But my parents continued the tradition of *ta moko* and my brothers and I all had this done when we turned sixteen. It was a rite of passage."

"I love it," she said. "Take your shirt off so I can see all of it." He did as she asked and felt her hands moving over the design. "Not tonight, but I might be able to find out more about your family and what tribe they belonged to. Each tattoo is distinctive to a different family."

"Definitely not tonight," he said. "But I'd love to know more about them."

She smiled up at him. "You constantly surprise me."

"How? You saw my birthmark—knew the Maori meaning. You had to guess I'd have some kind of body art," he said.

"If I'd thought about it, I would have. I wish I'd paid better attention when we were in the lake, but I was so focused on the moment and your kiss and not...well, not drowning."

"I wouldn't have let anything happen to you," he said. "My tattoo didn't come above the water level in the lake."

"No, it didn't," she said. "But it is still large."

She pushed his jeans and his boxers down his hips

and he had to maneuver the elastic of his waistband over his erection. Then his pants slid down to the floor and he turned so she could see the rest of the design.

It curved downward over his left buttock and then down his thigh. He shivered as sensations raced over his skin. She was fascinated by his tattoo. It was a part of him and he enjoyed her reaction to it. She knew the history and the importance of the ink on his skin and that made him like her even more.

He felt her fingers again on him, which made him shudder as she traced over his butt cheek before she cupped it and squeezed. He heard her hop off the console table and press against his back, wrapping her arms around him and taking his cock in her hand. She stroked him as he grew in her grip.

He felt her mouth against his back, dropping kisses between his shoulder blades as she worked him in her hand. He couldn't think anymore. All he could do was feel. Every breath he took was Jessie and her raw sexuality that left no room for anything but a powerful physical awareness of her.

He moaned and took her hand in his, turning around again to face her. He pushed his fingers into her hair, looking into her eyes. Something passed between them and he wanted to ignore it but couldn't. This was more than just sex.

She watched him carefully, as if she knew it, too. He noticed the pink flush of passion on her skin and he took a deep breath, the scent of wildflowers and sex heavy in the air.

He lowered his head and rubbed his lips over hers before nibbling kisses along the line of her jaw. He whispered into her ear all the things he wanted to do to her and she tightened her grip on his waist. Pulled him closer to her.

Rubbing his hands up and down her back, he pushed her panties down her legs and off, and then lifted her onto the console table again. He swept her sports bra over her head.

Her nipples tightened as he looked at her. She leaned back against the wall, her head at an angle to study him as he skimmed his gaze over her body. She parted her legs and he was captivated by the neatly trimmed light brown hair between them.

He felt the strength of her muscles as he caressed her thighs. She parted her legs further and shifted her hips forward.

Her skin was soft and tan, reminding him of the earth once more. She spent her time outside, exploring the planet, while he spent all of his time reaching for the cosmos. He wanted her, and the lust rode him hard. But in the back of his mind he knew they were very different people.

He shoved that thought aside and leaned down to kiss her belly button. She put her hands in his hair; he loved the feel of her fingers on his scalp as she subtly pushed his head lower.

He nibbled his way down to her intimate flesh, kissing the line at the top of her groin and then moving to her thigh. He bit her hip bone and saw gooseflesh spread down her leg. Slowly he kissed his way down her leg, lingering to lick the sensitive skin behind her knee before moving back up to her slick entrance. He parted her with his thumb and forefinger.

Her clit was engorged and tempting. He leaned

over her, teasing her with strokes of his tongue and using his other hand to trace the opening. He pushed his finger into her as he suckled her clit. His shoulders stung as she dug her nails into them, held him to her as she arched her hips into the motion of his finger and his mouth.

Her sensual moans filled the room and she surrounded him. The feel of her legs draped over his shoulders, the taste of her in his mouth, the moistness of her on his fingers—so addictive. He was hot and hard, so ready for her, but he wanted to give her this first. To bring her to pleasure, to hear the sounds she made for him. Only for him.

She arched frantically against his mouth and then let out a long, low cry. He gentled his touch and stood up, wiping his mouth with the back of his hand and leaning over her, bracing his hands on the table next to her hips. She wrapped her arms around his torso and rested her head against his racing heart.

He moved closer, the tip of his cock slipping between her legs, and she shifted so that he was poised at her entrance. He moved his hips forward and pushed himself deep inside her until he was fully seated. She tipped her head back and drew his head down to hers. Their mouths met and their tongues tangled as he started to move. He wanted to keep it slow and steady but there was a fire in his veins for her.

Everything primal rose up and he wanted to claim her. It didn't matter that a part of him wasn't sure she'd ever really be his, he was marking her as such. So that even when he was going where no one from

Earth had gone before, she'd always remember him
and this moment.

He tore his mouth from hers and pistoned his hips,
driving himself into her with a frantic need that felt as
if it would never be quenched. He tangled his hand in
her hair again, drew her head back and stared down
at her face. Her eyes were half-lidded, her mouth was
open and the flush of sex was on her skin.

She reached around to his back, her nails digging
into his buttocks, and that drove him over the edge.
He came hard and fast, thrusting into her three more
times to empty himself completely. He felt her tightening around him and she cried out his name.

He closed his eyes and rested his forehead on the
wall behind her, sheltering her body under his. He
swept his hands down her back, soothing her and
soothing himself. Slowly returning to this moment.
He waited until his breathing had calmed before he
opened his eyes and looked down at her face.

Eyes wide open, she smiled at him. His heart
clenched and he hugged her close.

"Well, um…"

He smiled at her, feeling light. Like for once he
could breathe and not worry about what would happen next. "Um…that sort of sums it up."

"Want to stay the night?" she asked. "It's okay if
you say no."

"Is it really okay?" he asked.

"Isn't it?"

"No. I want to stay the night. To hold you close
and, well, cuddle."

"Me, too," she said. "But I don't want to make
things awkward."

It was funny. She'd been so confident before, but now that they were facing each other in the aftermath, she seemed shy.

"It's not awkward. Well, it sort of is. I have to clean up a bit."

She smiled at him and then threw her head back. "I love how on TV and in movies this part is never a big deal. But in real life…"

"Yeah, in real life it's one of those things that has to be dealt with," he said.

"Okay, so, the bathroom is down the hall, second door on the right," she said, kissing his shoulder. "I'm going to clean up and I'll meet you back here."

He grabbed his jeans and walked toward the bathroom. Words weren't coming to him right now. Should he say something else? She seemed cool with just letting things ride and he wanted to be, too.

But this was Jessie.

The one who wouldn't give him any peace even when they were apart. He wanted to say something.

He turned around but she'd disappeared quietly.

He got to the bathroom and cleaned up, put his jeans back on and splashed water on his face. When he came out, he heard her singing off-key and followed the sound to the kitchen, where she had an iron teakettle and two mugs waiting.

"What's this?"

"Homemade hot chocolate. My mom's secret recipe. I only make it on special occasions," she said.

"I'm honored."

"You should be," she said. "I have a swing on the back porch. Want to meet me out there?"

He walked outside and sat down on the two person garden swing. It smelled new, the wood freshly cut, and took his weight easily. He kicked off with his feet, staring through the sparse cedar trees to the sky. From the time he was young, he'd noticed the way the sky changed with the seasons, the patterns of the stars. He'd been sickly for a while as a child and had spent six months inside, dreaming that one day he'd be here. Be a part of NASA.

"Here you go," she said, sitting down next to him on the swing and handing him a mug.

He looked over at her. For the first time in his life, someone was competing with the dream that was so deeply rooted in him—he couldn't remember a time when he didn't want to be up there in the stars. Out there in the universe, far away from this Earth.

"What are you thinking?"

He wanted to tell her, but he had a feeling he'd scare her off. And he wasn't sure what he wanted from her, not really. This feeling was so new to him. Maybe it wasn't real. How could it be? It didn't matter that his father had said he knew he'd marry Hemi's mother the day they met. Things like that no longer happened.

"This is the first time I've had homemade hot chocolate," he said.

"I hope you like it," she said.

He took a sip, and it was different, but as he sat on the swing with Jessie curled into his side, both of them sipping the hot chocolate and staring at the night sky, he found the peace that had eluded him since they met. He might not have all the answers, but for tonight this was enough.

She told him stories about the sea and different

7

WHEN JESSIE WOKE UP, Hemi was gone, which really didn't surprise her. He'd been quiet last night and so had she. Sex for sex's sake made sense to her, because it was a need. A basic, primal need.

And they had to work together, so making this into anything other than that basic need had "bad idea" written all over it. She was finding it harder to put him in a separate box.

But she couldn't get him out of her mind on her morning hike. She started out walking, music blasting from her earbuds. Then she ran, her feet driving into the ground, but no matter how fast she went she couldn't get away from the truth.

Hemi. And Alexi.

But unlike Alexi, this man wouldn't die on her. She got back to her cabin, showered and dressed in her NASA uniform. Then, instead of going to the training facility, she went to her computer and placed a video call to her parents.

They were somewhere in the Indian Ocean for her father's research into the migratory patterns of sharks. When he was done, they would move to the South Pacific to follow bioluminescent organisms, which was her mother's field of study. Jessie didn't bother to calculate the time difference because her mother had insomnia and was always up.

The call connected and a moment later her mom's face appeared on the screen. Jessie felt tears sting the backs of her eyes.

It had been so long since she'd seen her parents in person. Jessie knew she could fly to wherever they were to seek comfort and help for her sense of loss, but that would have felt like failure. So, instead, she'd taken this job in Texas to prove she was an adult and didn't need to go home.

"Baby girl," her mom said, by way of greeting. "How's Texas?"

"Hot," Jessie said. "Not the worst I've experienced, but it's hot."

"How's NASA?"

"Good. I love the work I'm doing and it seems like I'm really teaching these candidates something. Which feels great, because it's not like they haven't already lived remarkable lives."

They chatted for a few minutes, and after she finished talking to her mom, Molly called and asked Jessie if she could help her ride fences. One of the hands had been thrown earlier and they were shorthanded.

"Ace mentioned you some free time today," Molly said, "but if you'd rather not—"

"No. I need to get outside. I'll be right there. But I'm not sure I know what 'riding fences' means."

"It's just where we ride along the fence line and check to make sure the posts aren't loose and that the fence is still secure," Molly explained once Jessie arrived at the barn.

"I can't ride a horse," Jessie said.

"That's okay, we can take the Mule," Molly said, leading the way to the all-terrain vehicle. "Grab a hat from the wall."

Jessie donned a straw cowboy hat and joined Molly. Her friend put the vehicle in gear and they bounced over the pasture.

"We haven't had much time to chat lately. How're things?" Molly asked, when they were walking along the fence line.

"Not too bad," Jessie said. She wasn't ready to talk about Hemi. Not yet. "Why do you need a second person to do this?"

"Technically speaking, I don't. But this is the part of the ranch where Dad had his accident, and I didn't want to come out here alone," Molly said.

Molly's father, Mick Tanner, had been killed in an all-terrain vehicle accident while checking the fences. His death had been shocking to everyone, doubly so when he'd left the Bar T to Molly and Ace McCoy. Ace had been the one to suggest they bid to have some of the ranch land used for a NASA training facility.

"That's the best reason of all, to me," Jessie said. "Grief has a way of sneaking up on you when you least expect it."

Molly stopped and hopped out to check one of the posts. Jessie did the same.

"Is it easier being away from the Himalayas?" Molly asked. "Dad's everywhere on this ranch. See this brand on the fence post and how it's crooked?"

Jessie leaned around her friend. "Yeah."

"Dad made me laugh as I placed the brand on the post and it slipped," Molly said.

Jessie hugged the other woman close. "It's not easier being away. Sometimes when I'm running in the morning I think I can hear Alexi running beside me. I look around…"

Molly hugged her back. "This fence looks good. Let's talk about something cheery."

"I've been catching up on all the TV I missed while I was climbing," Jessie said. "I'm addicted to reality shows. So much drama."

Molly laughed and they chatted about the Real Housewives of different cities. When they got back to the barn, Jessie said, "Thank you. I needed an afternoon like this."

Molly nodded. "I needed it, too. Everyone is so intense at the training facility. I've been afraid to reach out and just say, 'Hey, want to hang?' Because that's not mission critical."

Jessie understood that. Everyone, herself included, was very aware of how focused they had to be on the timeline. NASA answered to the government and its private investing partners. They simply couldn't miss any deadlines.

"Mission critical? Who says that?" Jessie asked. But in her heart she already knew. A guy like Hemi would say that.

"Ace. I swear sometimes I don't know that man at all," Molly said.

"You know him pretty well," Jessie said. "In the ways that are important."

"I hope so," Molly said. "What's up with you and Hemi?"

"I don't know. I'm sort of trying to keep things low-key…"

"How's that working out for you?" Molly asked, affection and teasing in her tone.

"Not at all like I planned. He is so different. He has *ta moko*—this Maori tattoo he received when he was sixteen, as a rite of passage. And he is fearless when it comes to everything. He almost died in space, but he can't wait to go back up there and I…I didn't even fall on that last Everest attempt and I can't make myself go back. I just don't know what to do."

She felt a stirring of emotion, grief for Alexi, for herself. She wished she could return to when she believed that she would never lose her faith in herself.

"I'm not sure what to tell you. These astronauts are different. They dare to do things without a safety net. You know what that's like," Molly said.

"I used to," Jessie said.

"You will again," Molly said. "You're one of the strongest women—scratch that—one of the strongest *people* I know."

Her smartphone pinged and she grimaced as she checked it. "I have a meeting over at the training facility. Want a ride back to your place?"

Jessie took Molly up on her offer. Sitting in the all-terrain vehicle with the wind blowing on her face, it was easy to forget about her worries for a little while. But Hemi wasn't one to stay out of her thoughts.

She knew he was drawn to danger. The Mars mission was probably on his mind most of the time and she needed…she wanted stability. She'd already lost one lover. Alexi and she had had years together and that bond had developed over time.

But Hemi...well, Hemi took over her thoughts completely. It wasn't time or familiarity that drew them together, but the opposite.

"Drop me here," Jessie said. She wasn't ready to go to the facility right now.

Molly stopped the vehicle and Jessie got out. "See ya later."

She walked away from her friend, very aware that she wasn't any closer to finding answers than she had been earlier. But she felt lighter.

She actually had about twenty minutes before she needed to be in her classroom, so she emailed an anthropologist friend and asked for some information on traditional Maori tattoos.

Her mom's advice had been to ride this thing—both her grief and her attraction to Hemi, which she couldn't control, but it was hard to let go and just go with it. That wasn't her nature. People died when there wasn't a plan. When she wasn't in control. And it wasn't that caring for Hemi would put him in danger, it was that she hated to start something with him if it was only going to end.

HEMI TOOK HIS water bottle and sat down next to Ace, who was reviewing footage from the exploration satellite. The probe had been sent to the area between Earth and Mars where NASA was going to place the way station in orbit around the Sun.

"Damn, sometimes I feel like we are living in *Star Trek*," Hemi said.

"Me, too. I have to pinch myself sometimes to believe it's real," Ace said. "When I think about how close I came to not being assigned to the Cronus mission…"

Hemi clapped a hand on his friend's back. "But you did it. Your recovery is ongoing and you've really set some good markers for the rest of us. I know that Dr. Tomlin spends most of her time measuring my stats against yours. Hardly seems fair, since you don't have these guns."

Hemi flexed his arms, which made Ace laugh.

"Molly doesn't seem to mind."

"Nah, she thinks you're the bomb. Are you going to marry her before the first mission?" Hemi asked. Sleeping with Jessie…well, it had changed something fundamental inside of him and now he was thinking about what leaving her behind would be like. He knew if he got the open spot, he'd leave. And if he didn't make it, there would be a backup team that would train. He wanted to be on the A team. But could he achieve that goal when his attention was divided?

"Yes. I'd marry her tomorrow, but Rina said that we deserved a real nice wedding."

Rina was the housekeeper at the Bar T Ranch and was close to Molly. She'd been a constant in Molly's life after her mom had died.

"'Course you do."

"There's a new wedding planner in Cole's Hill who works for bigwigs like professional football players, European royalty and celebrities. Rina thinks we should use them," Ace said. "So stay lookin' good, best man, you're going to have to be part of a lot of pictures."

"Best man?" Hemi asked.

"Yeah, unless you don't want to," Ace said. "But you're my best friend so…"

"I'd love to, man. I'd be honored," Hemi said. "I'm really stoked about you and Molly. She's the perfect woman for you."

Ace nodded. "Don't let her hear you say that. She already thinks she knows more than me."

"Does she?"

"Yeah. Most of the time she's right. She's got a good intuition about people."

"What does she think of Jessie?" Hemi asked.

He hadn't planned on bringing her up, but the woman was on his mind. He wouldn't mind getting some advice from his friend, but his potential commander might see Jessie as a distraction.

"She likes her. They've been friends since childhood. Molly calls Jessie one of her 'she-roes.' She's done so much and Molly's never really left the ranch," Ace said. "I told her there are different kinds of strength."

"That's true," Hemi said. He sometimes forgot the difference between how people viewed him and how he felt inside. But it reassured him that Molly saw what he did in Jessie. She was just going through a rough patch. Had he helped or hurt her?

It was hard to regret a night like the one he'd shared with her, but she was slowly wrapping herself around his heart and it was difficult not to worry about her. She had seemed fragile when she'd fallen asleep in his arms. He'd held her, watched her. Seeing that strength quieted had brought out protective instincts that had surprised him.

"What's going on with the two of you?" Ace asked. "Should I be worried you're not going to be the top of your group?"

"Nah. I got that. I'm outdoing myself during the tests, and my strength is ridiculous right now. I spent forty-five minutes on the space station simulator treadmill this morning and showed my best time and vitals."

"That's physical stuff. What about the emotional part?" Ace asked. "Is she in your head?"

Hemi leaned back in the chair, staring up at the ceiling in the darkened projection room. "Hell, I want to tell you no, so you won't think I'm unfocused, but the truth is…she's different, Ace. I can't explain it. If I'd met her at any other time in my life it would be better. But she's here now and I can't just walk away."

Ace laughed and Hemi glanced over at him.

"Mick used to say that women were one of the mysteries of life that men would never be able to unravel."

Mick had been the closest thing to a dad that Ace had had. And that advice was about as good as any Hemi's father or older brothers had given him.

Hemi didn't know how to handle whatever was happening inside of him because of Jessie. She had erased all of his preconceptions last night and if he'd thought that whatever was between them was just physical, well, he'd scratched that itch but he still wanted her. He needed more. He'd been thinking about her all day—had spent as long as he had in the gym trying to force his mind onto something else. But all he could see was Jessie beside him. With him.

He wanted her. Still.

Most of the time he had a pretty even sex drive. He could go a few days without it when he didn't have a woman in his life. But with Jessie he was thinking about getting her naked under him again. And then again. He wanted her more than he'd ever wanted anything except his spot on this mission.

He had to get this under control.

"What are you looking at?" Hemi asked. "I know you said satellite footage but is this the location where we'll build the way station?"

"Yeah. We're debating between two different locations. I think you found some anomalies near one of them."

Hemi leaned closer to the large monitor. He watched the sky looking for the kind of disturbances that would prohibit them from safely putting in the way station.

"Yes," he said, tapping the screen. "Close to the asteroid belt. But the team and I have done some analysis and we think it looks good. Will you be reporting these findings to the group?"

"Yes. I want you guys to be looking for problems I might not see," Ace said.

Hemi was looking forward to having something other than Jessie to think about.

MOLLY AND RINA had invited all the women at the NASA facility to a "ladies' night." Molly had billed it as a book club but the email invite said it was a chance to get together and share some girl talk.

Jessie had debated long and hard about going. She wasn't naturally social but she needed to get out of her own head. Her mother's advice hadn't really helped. But, then, her mom had spent most of her time studying people and liked to see situations unfold. At times it had made Jessie's life a little difficult.

She put on a pair of loose-fitting linen pants that she'd gotten at a bazaar in India and a loose-necked cotton T-shirt. Two of the Cronus candidates, Izzy and Mel, were on the path toward the main ranch house.

"Hey, Jessie," Izzy said. She wore a pair of Western-style boots and a denim skirt. "Getting my cowgirl on tonight."

"I got mine on earlier when I rode fences. This part of the facility feels like a training campus, but then, as soon as I see the barn and hear the horses, I know I'm on a ranch in Texas," Jessie said.

"Me, too," Mel said. "They've had us doing round-ups and I'm sore. That's a whole set of muscles I've never used."

Jessie laughed. They continued down the path. "I'm not sure what this will be like. I haven't been to a girls' night…ever."

Mel laughed and shook her head. "It's been a while for me, too. Work always takes precedence over downtime, but I'm looking forward to this."

"Me, too. I heard the guys are having a poker night," Izzy said. "I've played with them a few times."

"Me, too. Hemi has a world-class poker face," Mel said.

Jessie listened to the other women and realized that the candidates were like a family. They knew each other pretty well and acted almost like siblings. A part of her—the womanly, confused part—wanted to probe and ask questions about Hemi.

But she really didn't want to reveal too much of what was going on between them. She wasn't ready for that to be public.

"Do you ever play poker?" Mel asked. "I'm not sure what you do when you're climbing Everest."

"Well, we do play cards sometimes. You have to climb up to different base camps and then spend time acclimating to the altitude. Usually we have a running poker game. I don't really have a poker face."

"That's probably a good thing in your business," Izzy said. "I know I wouldn't want to have to guess if you were telling me the truth about a situation."

"Yeah. But it can also suck when I know things are going to shit."

"I know what you mean. I'm not really good at bluffing, either. One time I was on the ISS and we had a malfunction with the life-support system. I was supposed to just keep calm, do my part and get it repaired. Which I totally did, but the others could see I was rattled," Mel said, tucking a strand of her brown hair behind her ear. "I think I was so focused on getting the repair done I couldn't think of pretending nothing was going on."

"That's not a bad a thing, Mel. Everyone said you were cool and calm during the repair," Izzy said.

"Thanks," Mel said.

"That's the thing," Jessie said. "Just making sure that everyone is safe, regardless of what they know about the condition."

"That's what I'm getting from your lessons. You seem to always be in control. No matter what's going on," Izzy said. "Is that a skill you were able to develop? I hope the answer is yes, otherwise I think I might be doomed."

Izzy was one of the top candidates in the program and Jessie doubted she was ever going to be doomed. "It is something I developed. A lot of the time, people have an expectation of what you can do and what you are bringing to the table. So you guys see someone who has survived many dangerous adventures—you see me as in control. But the truth is I'm just as... well, normal—for lack of a better word—as everyone else. I'm not nearly as together as you both seem to think I am."

Mel laughed. "That is so reassuring. I really panicked in the first test when it kept getting colder. I'm just not used to dealing with extremes in temperature."

"But you didn't panic when you were in space. Sometimes the test environment doesn't play to everyone's strengths. Knowing you're in a test environment affects how some react. That's why we used the break room and we will continue changing up the tests."

"Good to know," Izzy said.

They arrived at the ranch house and walked up the steps to the wide porch with its big wooden rockers. The door opened as they approached and Molly waved them inside.

"You three are the last to arrive. I've got drinks and food set up out on the deck by the pool."

Jessie followed the other women through the house and outside. As she got to talking, she found the evening to be relaxing and different than what she'd expected. Once she stopped worrying about being awkward, she wasn't anymore.

Most of the women wanted to know about her adventures and she enjoyed sharing them. Talking about her past reconnected her to the stories in a way she hadn't felt since Alexi's death.

She'd lost more than she had realized when he'd slipped and fallen to his death. Her guilt had made her question choices she'd made and the path she'd always been on. Rationally, she knew Alexi's fall had been an accident, but she was plagued by fears. If her reaction had been quicker or if she'd done something differently, maybe she could have saved him. That was one of the things that concerned her about her trainees. She didn't want to fail them. But as they all talked and laughed, she felt her fears easing.

As she walked back toward her cabin afterward, she found herself looking at the converted bunkhouses. She had no idea which room was Hemi's, but she missed him and she wished that she hadn't been avoiding him all day.

All day she'd been afraid to let him in, but when she saw the shadowy figure waiting on her cabin's porch she realized she already had.

8

HEMI HAD LOST at poker. That rarely happened, which just underscored how distracted he was by Jessie. He wasn't making smart choices. And it had to end. But as he sat on her porch waiting for her return, he'd had time to think.

He realized how much better he thought when he was outside. He had leaned against the porch railing and looked up at the night sky, finding his balance once again.

If this were an affair, that would be one thing. But with Jessie, everything felt more extreme. He was telling himself she could be the one, but a part of him was starting to wonder if it was fear driving him.

Jessie mattered to him. Despite what he'd been trying to prove to himself—that she wasn't distracting him—he had to admit she was. And now he was afraid she might be changing him. He'd always liked being single, but he wasn't too sure he wanted to be alone anymore. His buddies at NASA were married or in committed relationships, his brothers were starting to settle down and he was still bumping along trying to make sense of his life the way he had in his twenties.

He saw Jessie walking toward him. Her blond hair was pulled back, making her features more prominent.

She was distracting him, and for the good of the mission he should be the one to end it. *Do it tonight and do it cleanly.*

"Hello."

His voice seemed too loud in the quiet night.

"Hemi. I didn't expect to see you tonight," she said.

"Me, either. But I... We need to talk," he said.

She nodded, brushing past him and taking a key from her pocket. Her clothing seemed to accentuate her slender, fit body and he felt that rush of awareness of her.

She unlocked her front door and then glanced back at him. "Want to come in?"

"Yes," he said. Though he questioned the wisdom of that decision as soon as they were in the hallway. He remembered how she'd looked sitting naked on the console table.

He swallowed hard as he followed her down the hall into her kitchen.

"Drink?"

"Just water," he said.

She poured two glasses from a filter pitcher and they sat at the butcher-block kitchen table.

She put her arms on the table, holding her glass loosely between her hands.

"What did you want to talk about?" she asked.

Suddenly all the words he'd had in mind were

gone. He didn't want to say that it was time for good-bye. He wanted more.

Until he saw her it had been easy to forget that he wanted her. That he needed her. But sitting across from her, it was more difficult to deny the truth.

"I don't know," he said.

"Seriously?"

"Yeah. I had thought…well, it doesn't matter. I thought I was coming over here tonight to say we should call it quits, but then I saw you and I realized I wanted to know how your day was. I know you had classes and you can't talk to me about the other candidates, but I wanted to know how you are doing," he admitted. "Not say goodbye."

She shook her head, looking down into her water glass like she was trying to divine the future from it. "I wish it were easier to figure out what to do with you, Hemi. I like you and I wasn't expecting that."

That surprised a laugh out of him. "Sorry?"

She glanced up from under her lashes. "Not at all. It's just I thought this thing between us would be… an affair."

"And you're upset it's not."

"Let's just say it would be a hell of a lot easier if it were," she said. "You're not my usual kind of guy."

He pushed his chair back on two legs and balanced it with his feet on the floor. "I guess you needed someone different."

She nodded. "What about you? Why are you here tonight?"

"Same. I have spent the entire day trying to keep what happened between us last night in perspective, but I can't seem to stop thinking about you. Even when I'm working, you're there in my mind."

"What are we going to do?"

Hemi put his chair down and leaned forward, stretching his arms across the table until he could take her hands in his. He held them for a long time, staring down at their fingers. "I can't pretend like there is nothing between us. If you feel differently…"

He looked up at her waiting for her response.

She shook her head and he let out a sigh. He hadn't realized how much he'd hoped for just that response.

"Okay, I'd like to try dating," he said. "I mean, we're both working at the facility every day, and that has to stay professional, but in the evenings and on our days off, could we try getting to know each other better?"

She pulled her hands from his and rubbed her palms over her upper arms. "I'm willing to try it," she said at last. "But I don't think I've ever really dated."

"Good, then everything we do will be new," he said. "I have a late start tomorrow. Do you have a morning class?"

The trainees were split into different groups for different kinds of training, so she didn't always see Hemi with the same group of people.

"Not until ten," she said.

"Great. Will you go for a morning ride with me?" he asked. "We can have a picnic breakfast."

She nibbled on her bottom lip. "I can cook for us here."

"I want to do this. It will be fun," he said.

She took a deep breath and then let it out. "I don't know how to ride."

"What? I thought you knew everything," he said.

"Well, I don't," she admitted.

"I can teach you or we can take my pickup. The place I wanted to picnic is on the ranch property and I can easily drive us there."

"Okay, if you don't mind driving," she said, "I'm happy to go along."

He pushed his chair back and stood up from the table. "Then I'll say good-night."

She got up and followed him to the door; she stood a few feet from him, clearing her throat when he reached for the handle.

"Yes?" he asked, looking back at her.

"Aren't you going to kiss me good-night?" she asked.

"I'm afraid if I kiss you, I'll still be here in the morning," he said.

JESSIE WOKE UP just before six and got dressed for the early morning picnic with Hemi. She'd told herself she was okay that he'd left without kissing her, but she wasn't.

She dressed in a pair of khaki cargo pants and a lightweight sweater and went out on the porch to wait for him.

He arrived ten minutes later with a leather backpack and a thermos loosely held in his other hand. He had a pair of well-worn jeans, a chambray button-down shirt and a Stetson.

Her breath caught in her throat. He looked like a cowboy. The sexy, rugged, save-a-horse, ride-a-cowboy type.

"I left my truck over by the barn," he said, his voice a deep rumble in the early morning.

Struggling to keep her hands to herself and not pull him to her, she made a noncommittal sound.

"You sure I can't change your mind about riding a horse?" he asked.

"I'm not," she admitted. "You look like you belong here on the Bar T."

"Well, my pops grew up dreaming of the American West and being a dude on a dude ranch, so every summer we went to Montana and learned to be cowboys."

"Why am I just now hearing this?" she asked, falling into step beside him as they headed toward the main ranch facilities. "I sometimes forget we're on a ranch."

"Me, too. That's why I wanted to try to get out with you this morning. I've been in Texas for most of my adult life but spend much of it inside a simulator."

"I haven't really spent much time in Texas prior to this, but I've been enjoying learning about the land. Every time I think I've seen all it has to offer, I spot something else."

"Really? Like what?"

"I found a new wash yesterday when I was hiking. With some deep trenches in the earth," she said. "I always enjoy that."

"Sounds interesting. Maybe you can show it to me sometime."

"Maybe," she said. "Let's see how this dating thing goes."

"Think you might get bored with me?"

Never. "Who knows? But we might not have as much in common as we hope."

"Do you hope we do?" he asked.

She wasn't sure what he was asking her. It would be easier to have taken him back to bed. But she had the feeling sex wasn't going to bring her the answers she wanted about Hemi. Though a part of her, the primal part, thought *to hell with that*. Sex with Hemi was never a bad idea.

"I'm not sure. I mean, Alexi and I trained together every day, lived together when we weren't hiking, and it made sense that we were lovers. We just fit each other's lives. But you and I, Hemi, we're very different."

He didn't say anything else for a long time and Jessie wondered if she'd been too blunt. It wasn't in her nature to hedge, but perhaps this time she should have.

"Did I say the wrong thing?" she asked.

"No. You were honest and that's what I wanted from you. I was just wondering how I could compete with a man who matched you in every way."

She had no answer to that. She didn't want to admit to herself that Hemi already had Alexi beat because he made her feel more alive than Alexi ever had. She was beginning to think that the appeal of Alexi was that he was her partner on her daring adventures. Not one of the crew members but her partner.

Hemi was an adventure in himself. But was she up for the voyage?

She didn't have to be doing something dangerous to feel exhilarated around him.

That worried her. What would happen after they got to know each other?

Was this all going to fade?

His truck was parked in front of the barn and he hesitated next to the big Chevy Silverado. "So...can I talk you into an early morning ride?"

She took a deep breath. Maybe riding a horse would give her the distraction she needed. A chance to get out of her head and just enjoy the morning with him.

"Is there a horse gentle enough for a first-time rider?" she asked.

He smiled at her and her heart beat a little faster. She hadn't realized how much that genuine smile would change his face and she knew in that moment that no matter what, there was already more than sex between her and the big Maori astronaut.

"I'm sure we can find one for you," he said, holding his hand out to her.

As their fingers entwined, she had a flashback to Alexi and how she'd been holding him, using all of her strength to keep him from falling into the crevasse on Everest. She let her hand drop and stepped back, only this time it was Hemi hanging on to her.

"Jess?"

"Sorry, Hemi. I just...let's get on with this ride," she said. She needed to do something to get her mind away from the past.

"What is it that you see when you turn as white as a ghost?" he asked.

"I see my biggest nightmare," she admitted.

"And that is?"

"Not being strong enough to do what has to be done," she said, walking past him into the large barn.

The smell of hay and the sound of horses was foreign to her, but soothing. Hemi came in behind her and gave her directions for saddling her horse, his voice calm and soothing.

She didn't dwell on the memory of Alexi, didn't want to, but in the back of her mind was the fact that she was starting to fear losing Hemi. And that wasn't a good place to be.

9

HEMI HAD SPOKEN to Ace last night about the possible trail ride. Ace had told him that if he changed his mind about taking the truck there were a couple of horses that were trail mates, perfect for riding. Hemi had already been out on Rusty, and there was a docile mare that Ace had suggested for Jessie. Her name was Daisy. As they saddled up and left the barn, Hemi knew that Daisy was the right horse for Jessie. The mare followed his horse easily.

Something had happened before they entered the barn and he'd made up his mind to give her space. He wanted to push. He wasn't the kind of man to sit back and let things ride. He never had been.

But his instincts were telling him that he needed to keep his mouth shut and let the morning quiet help Jessie.

They left the barn and busy ranch area and took the path that led toward an old homestead cabin that Ace had told Hemi about. Jessie held herself stiffly at first, but as the ride went on she started to relax in the saddle.

She came abreast of him and he glanced over at her. "You okay?"

"Yeah. I wanted to apologize for being so—"

"Don't. There's nothing to apologize for," he said.

She nodded.

He reached out his hand, and she took a deep breath and took it. Their horses continued their slow walk and they held hands in the companionable silence. But Hemi could feel the tension in her.

"Why does holding hands bother you?" he asked, when they arrived at the cabin and brought their horses to a stop.

She let go of his hand to dismount and he followed suit. "Ace said the horses are trained to stay if you put their reins on the ground."

She dropped the reins for her horse and walked toward the cabin, which, according to Ace, was not in use.

Hemi took the thermos of tea from his saddlebag and followed her to the porch, where she sat on one of the rough-hewn steps.

"So…"

"I was holding on to Alexi when he fell. I'd anchored my line and then reached down to try to grab him, and he slipped from me. We weren't roped together because balance can be affected when crossing a crevasse. We both liked to be more independent when climbing. And when I held your hand, when you reached for me earlier, I had a weird flashback."

"I'm sorry."

She shrugged. "It's just I thought I couldn't be farther away from the incident than here in Texas. That my memories were fading, so it surprised me."

He shrugged out of his backpack and opened it, taking out the enamel mugs he'd brought with him for their tea.

"It happens," Hemi said.

"Not to you," she countered, taking the mugs and thermos from him and pouring them both a cup of tea.

"Yes, to me. One time when I was in Houston at the Natural Buoyancy Laboratory—"

"What's that?"

"It's an aquatic facility where we don space suits and are submerged into water to simulate space walks," he said, pushing his cowboy hat a bit to get a better look at her face. "They're building one here, as well. It will be ready for the phase two training."

"What will they use the facility here for? There's so much going on with the training of the candidates and I've been focused on my part and not really paid attention to the second phase."

"To practice putting together the way station module. That's going to be some fun." Hemi couldn't wait to get the module here on-site so they could start working with it.

"Sounds interesting," she said. "What happened to you when you were in there in Houston?"

"I had this odd flash. I was in the simulator with Izzy and we were supposed to be lifting a repair arm when it slipped from my grip and she couldn't duck out of the way. It hit her helmet and jarred her, but when I reached for her hand to steady her, I freaked a little because our hands didn't connect and she drifted from me. I knew we were in the pool but it also felt, well…real."

She nodded. "That's how it is for me. I've had traumatic things happen in the past and never had this kind of problem."

Hemi leaned back on his elbows, stretching his legs along the steps. Past lovers were at the bottom of the list of things he wanted to know more about. But he remembered something his father had said a long time ago, when he and his brothers had started dating. He said loving someone meant accepting everything in their past, and that included the people who'd broken their hearts. Hemi wasn't sure if Alexi's death had broken Jessie's heart, but he could see that it had broken something inside of her.

"Do you feel guilty?"

She put her elbows on her knees and rested her head in her hands. She stared down at her feet, shoulders hunched. Hemi sat up and rubbed her neck.

"If you need to talk, I'm here," he said. "I've been told I'm a pretty good listener."

She shook her head and her silky hair brushed over his hand. "Nah, I don't want to talk."

"What do you want to do?" he asked. "I've got a very healthy yogurt parfait for each of us and some trail mix bars that are supposed to help with bone density."

She looked over at him and gave him the shadow of her normal smile, but he realized he was doing the right thing. Ignoring the issue instead of facing it head-on went against his instinct, but this was how she wanted to deal with her problem. He was trying to remind himself that they were out here together to see if there would be an "us" and then he could help her face her fears and move on.

SHE WAS RESTLESS, and sitting this close to Hemi after realizing how vulnerable he made her feel, well, it wasn't something she wanted to do. She pushed herself to her feet and ambled along the porch.

"Have they assigned anyone to live here?"

"Nope. Ace said it was the cabin that the Tanners originally used when the land was first granted to them. Molly is partial to it, so they excluded it from the training facility."

"I love that Molly's family has been here for that long," she said. "It was nice that NASA named the facility after Mick."

"It was. And since Mick was a large influence on Ace, I think it meant something to him that Dennis suggested it."

She turned to glance at Hemi where he sat sprawled on the steps. She put her arms on the worn wood railing and leaned heavily on it. "Death has a long-fingered grip. It touches so many things that you never realize."

"You are…" He trailed off.

Crazy. A downer. All of them applied to her this morning. She was taking her confusion with Hemi and channeling it into something she wasn't. She embraced life—or she used to.

"God, I'm sorry. I… I can't stand here and talk," she said. "Want to race?"

"Race?"

"Yeah. Race you to that tree…usually there's a reason why one tree is left on a prairie area like this. I asked Molly about it and she said it had been too big for her ancestors to uproot and they'd just left it."

"I like that," Hemi said, getting to his feet. "Big things are hard to move."

She knew he was referring to himself and the heavy mantle that had been on her shoulders all morning lifted. It was easier to breathe.

"Water and sun wear them away eventually," she said.

"But not one tiny girl."

"Tiny girl? Are you referring to me?" she asked. "I'm a five-foot-ten woman."

He shrugged. "I'm six-two. And I have a lot more muscles. You look tiny to me."

She laughed. Threw her head back and started laughing until the sound wouldn't stop and tears started rolling down her face. She tried to turn away but that didn't give her the distance she needed. She just started running, and the manic laughter died. As she raced across the plain, her booted feet falling heavily in the quiet of the early morning, everything faded. Her lungs burned as she tried to gulp in air and her leg muscles burned because she hadn't stretched or warmed up but she felt...

Alive.

It had been something she'd been able to achieve only in little bursts, and now it was here and it felt so damned real.

She heard Hemi a moment before she felt his hands on her waist. He lifted her as if she were the tiny girl he'd called her. Lifted her up over his shoulder and then spun around.

He shifted her gently into his arms. She looked up into his face again, saw that smile that made her heart beat a little faster, and she realized that she had almost missed out on the gift of this morning with Hemi. Not because of anything other than worry. Maybe it was just being here and working a regular job, but she was forgetting that everything moved on. She'd spent enough time in nature to know that worry never really changed anything substantial.

He tipped her backward slowly and she had to grab his shoulders and hold on. He was a big, solid man, and she lifted one hand, tracing the mark around his right eye. Then she let her fingers glide over his cheekbone to his mouth and down his neck.

He leaned down, his Stetson blocking the sun, and she felt the brush of his lips against her. Her mind stopped racing as her blood started. She held him closer to her, felt the sun on her arms and his body heat against her side.

He surrounded her and made everything else disappear. He tasted like the tea he'd brought for them to drink, minty toothpaste and Hemi.

That taste had become very familiar to her during the night they'd spent together. She realized all the running and thinking and analyzing hadn't done a thing to stop her from wanting him.

She pushed his hat from his head, running her fingers through his hair and holding him to her while she deepened the kiss. Their tongues tangled; she couldn't get enough of him and he knew it.

He slowly let her legs slide down and she stood there pressed against him, more secure now that she was on the ground. He wrapped one arm around her waist and lifted his head. Their eyes met and she realized that whatever was between them wasn't going to go away.

There was no running from it and she sensed in that moment that Hemi knew it, too.

But she remembered what had happened outside the barn. How she'd seen his face and felt him slip from her grip. Could she stop him from leaving? Could she insulate herself from being hurt? She didn't want to if it meant she'd have to let him go now.

She knew then that Hemi wasn't going to fit into any of the comfortable boxes she'd always used to catalogue the men in her life, and as she took his hand in hers, she knew that was okay.

For the first time since she'd come to Texas, she didn't feel lost. Little pieces of the woman she'd been were coming back to her but this time they were merging with who she was now.

"I'm ready for some of that breakfast now," she said.

"I'm ready for some of you," he said.

"Some of me?" she asked, running her finger down the center of his chest. "Not all of me?"

ALL OF HER. It was what he was struggling with. His studies at the Mick Tanner Training Facility were going well, but he knew that part of the reason for that was that he wanted to impress her. He wanted to be the biggest, baddest astronaut in the training program and he'd do whatever he had to in order to get her attention.

"Woman, you know I want all of you."

"What are you going to do about it? You caught me," she said, her voice confident, not like earlier when she'd been on the brink of something he hadn't been able to identify. He still wasn't sure what had happened and he wanted answers, wanted to barge through her barriers. But he knew if he pushed too hard she'd simply walk away. That was what she did.

He held her close. Just held on and enjoyed this moment with the morning sun over them, the Texas land all around them and the peace that he wasn't sure was real. But the woman was. He held her like he'd never let her go.

She lifted her face to the sun as a breeze blew around them and he buried his face in her neck. She smelled good, fresh and clean and like Jessie. He kissed the point where her neck and shoulder met. Felt her heart beat strongly there and then sucked gently on that spot until she tightened her arms around him.

He dropped butterfly kisses on her neck up to her jaw until she turned her head and their lips met. As always, when he kissed her, his body went into overdrive. She tasted of the morning and freedom, and again he had that feeling that if he didn't act quickly enough she'd slip through his fingers.

It was ironic that he was the one who'd be leaving if everything went as planned but she was the flight risk. She had said she didn't want to lose herself in him and he had no idea how to manage that. How he was going to keep her was still a mystery to him. And he was more a man of action than a man who could puzzle out secrets. His gut said *claim her.*

Never let her go.

He could do it.

She'd admitted that she was lost. He could show her a new way of life with him. Make her so completely his that...when he left she'd be lost again.

He could never do that.

The late summer grass was high and fragrant in the morning air, and he held her even closer. When they were apart he always thought that just holding her in his arms would be enough. But she was like a nebula—so damned breathtaking, but so distant.

Dammit.

He stopped letting his mind worry over the endless ways that this could go wrong and lowered his mouth to hers.

She tasted of dreams and hopes this morning. He knew he was projecting but hell, he'd rather taste that than the reality that waited for the both of them.

She was a strong, independent woman and he knew that whether he left on the first Cronus mission or a later one, she'd stay strong and move on.

Moving on…

He didn't want to her to do that. He wanted to keep her in some kind of stasis until he got back and could claim her again. But he was a realist. Why did Jessie make him want to believe in things that he knew weren't practical?

"You're looking really fierce. Much like your nickname… Thor. How'd you get that one?"

"I got struck by lightning on the golf course. Ace spread it around that I called down the thunder."

"Did you call down the thunder?" she asked.

He smiled. "I might have been talking shit right before it happened."

"Were you hurt?"

"Just a little tingling in my body, but nothing permanent."

She laughed and he felt that punch to his gut again.

He pulled her close and took the kiss he needed. He couldn't be gentle and seduce her slowly. He needed to bond with his mate. He looked around and knew they were hidden from view should anyone approach.

And there was no denying that Jessie was his mate. His.

He undid her jeans, shoving them down her legs while he kept their mouths fused. His tongue tangled with hers and her hands roamed up and down his back. Then he felt her hands on his crotch and his zipper was down. She freed him from his underwear before stroking her hand up and down his length.

His hips jerked forward and he knew he was on the edge.

He lifted her in his arms and sat down—inelegantly, but never losing his grip on her. He pulled her onto his lap so she straddled him, and her legs, hampered by her jeans, spread just far enough for him to nestle his cock up against her. She started pulling off her clothes, and he helped her, until her jeans and underwear lay in a heap next to them.

He drew her back onto his lap, and she settled over him, slowly lowering herself down his length until he was buried deep inside of her. She tipped her head back as she started to ride him. Her hair flowed around her shoulders and his heart caught. He watched her and realized how much this woman meant to him.

He put his hands on her hips, driving her faster and faster. She clutched at his shoulders, his name a litany from her lips, which intensified the feathery sensation down the small of his back. He wanted her to come first, and as he tried to hold on she leaned closer to him.

He felt the brush of her breath against his cheek. "I like your hammer, Thor."

A bark of laughter escaped him and he came at the same time. He held her tightly, felt her tightening around him and she threw her head back, riding him hard until they both were spent.

He held her close to him, stroked his hands up and down her back. But, like the sunrise, Hemi suspected that he wasn't going to be able to keep Jessie any longer than he could keep the dawn.

10

THE NOTE HAD simply read: *Meet me at the barn*. She'd had a long day working with one of the groups Hemi wasn't in. She'd put too much stress on her ankle pulling up a candidate who'd gone down near a fallen tree during a hike. She was hot, tired and more than a little cranky.

They'd both been very busy since they'd had their early morning picnic a week ago. Hemi's schedule was rigorous and she had been working with all the candidates as well as doing assessments for Dennis and Ace.

She looked at the note again, with its bold, block-style writing and his name at the bottom. There was an arrow, too, and when she flipped the paper over, she saw he'd written one more word on the back.

Please.

She smiled to herself. She couldn't resist that kind of invitation and he knew it. He had to know it.

She showered and changed into a skirt that she'd gotten in a market in Morocco and a light sweater that her mother had given her for Christmas two years ago. She wrapped her ankle with a Tensor bandage and then put on a pair of cowboy boots.

The walk to the barn wasn't too far and she enjoyed being by herself, though she wasn't sure she was up to riding. As much as she enjoyed teaching the classes at the training facility, she also enjoyed any pockets of time she could carve out for herself. As she got closer to the barn she noticed a restored '57 Chevy pickup with the tailgate down. Two cowboys were sitting on the tailgate, but from a distance she couldn't make out who they were.

As she approached, one of them got up and she saw it was Ace. He walked past, tipping his hat as he did so.

"Good evening, Jessie," he said, following the path that led up toward the house.

"Evening, Ace."

As she got closer she saw the other cowboy was Hemi. He hopped off the tailgate as she approached and put his hands on his hips.

He looked like he'd been born to ride the range with his faded jeans clinging to his thighs, those worn boots on his feet and the button-down plaid shirt that fit his muscled arms and shoulders like a second skin.

"I wasn't sure you were going to show," he said, holding his hand out to her.

"I wasn't sure, either," she admitted, taking his hand.

"Was there anything that tipped the odds in my favor?" he asked, leading her to the cab of the truck and opening the passenger side door for her.

"Saying *please*."

"I knew it. My mom says manners will open all

doors." Hemi stepped back so she could climb up into the cab. She sat on the blanket-covered bench seat and Hemi got behind the wheel.

"I was surprised to see you dressed like this," she said.

"Ace has us all on rotation on the ranch so we get out of the facility a couple of times a week. Some of the folks are placing solar panels out on an unused part of the ranch. I'm helping feed and tend to the herd with some of the others who like to ride. And then there are the roundups that we're all participating in. We've been working in different groups to see how we manage together."

She looked him over. Every time she thought she knew everything about him, he surprised her.

"Why are we heading to the old homestead?" she asked.

"Because I know you like to be alone and I wanted to be with you," he said.

A few simple words that summed her up. She was so isolated. And she'd been around Hemi enough to know he wasn't. He liked the company of others. He was always in conversation with someone.

"Why do you like me?" she asked, at last.

He took his eyes off the rutted dirt road and glanced over at her, his gaze skimming her body and his hand coming to rest on her thigh. "You're kidding, right?"

"So, it's just physical?" she asked, putting her hand on top of his and noting how much bigger his hand was than hers. She didn't want it to be just physical anymore, so she tried to make it seem like the answer didn't matter much to her.

"So far that's all you've allowed it to be."

"Touché."

She laced their fingers together and looked at him. The sun was setting and he'd turned his attention back to driving. His profile was strong and serious in the twilight.

"You make me wish I was different," she said.

He braked and turned to face her. "Don't. You are exactly who I want to be with."

She nodded. Hoped that was true. That she was enough. Not for Hemi, but for herself to be with Hemi. Was Hemi just a little bit of fun?

Though to call any part of him *a little bit* made her smile.

She looked away, noticing that the old homestead was glowing with light.

"What's that?"

"Just my surprise," he said, putting the truck back in gear and pulling up in front of the cabin.

But the light wasn't coming from the building. It was emanating from the back. She opened her door and hopped out as soon as Hemi had turned the engine off, and he came around, holding a bandanna.

"Hold on. You need to wear this blindfold."

She gave him a long level look. "Are you sure about this?"

He nodded. "I think you're going to have to trust me."

She turned around so he could tie the bandanna over her eyes, very aware that she did trust him. It was herself she had a hard time trusting.

"Follow me," he said, taking her hand.

Blindly she followed him, contemplating how easy it was to let him lead.

HE KNEW HE needed to make her see him in a different light. To show her there was more to him than just red-hot sex and muscles. And he needed something, too. Something with Jessie that would be a memory outside of the facility. But neither of them had time to leave. They might be able to take a day trip to NASA if he combined it with one of his medical tests, but the truth was the Bar T was pretty much it.

Hemi wasn't good at romance. But his brother, the one who used to play in the NFL, was. In fact, Manu had a reputation with the ladies that Hemi freely admitted he envied. So a quick call to his brother had netted this plan.

He glanced around at the gnarled old scrub oak that he'd spent most of the afternoon draping twinkling lights on. He was going to have to pull double duty on the ranch for a recruit who'd covered for him this afternoon, but it was worth it. Then he'd tied Mason jars holding tiny tea lights in the branches, lighting everything before going to wait for Jessie. He'd cut wood for the ground fire pit, and stacked blankets and pillows around the pit so they'd have a nice place to sit and enjoy their picnic dinner.

Molly had provided him with the blankets and Ace with a Bose speaker for his iPhone. All in all, it had taken a village to make this quiet, intimate dinner for Jessie. Hemi knew he was lucky in the people he called friends. They had come through for him so often.

He led Jessie to the blanket.

"Stand still," he said, leaving her for a moment to check on the sparkling water he had chilling and the food Rina had prepared. One thing he wasn't, and that was a chef.

Everything was perfect.

Jessie stood there with the red bandanna covering half her face and his breath still caught in his chest. She was the most beautiful woman he'd ever seen. Sometimes he found it hard to believe that she wanted to be with him.

True, she wanted it to just be sex, but he knew they were growing closer every day and it was truly much more than sex.

It had been for him from the beginning.

He walked back over, wanting to kiss her. But dammit, he had a plan. He'd gone to some effort to make tonight about more than sex. He wanted to get to know her.

And he'd always felt most comfortable under the stars. With the cosmos stretching out above them.

He wanted to share that with her. For the first time in his life he'd found someone who came close to competing with NASA and the space program. Normally the women he dated were fun. A nice break from his work life, but with Jessie…

"You're back."

"I am," he said. Maybe this was a mistake. But it didn't feel like it. He wanted them to grow closer.

Surely he could do that.

"I could feel your body heat," she said, lifting her hand to touch his arm. "Can I take the blindfold off?"

"Not yet."

"Why not?"

"Because this," he said, lowering his mouth to

hers and claiming a kiss that he hoped would be soft and romantic.

A Hollywood kiss, because that was what this setting and this woman deserved. Her lips parted under his and her tongue darted into his mouth. He groaned, tasting the mint of her toothpaste and something else.

Her nails dug into his biceps and she teetered forward. He wrapped one arm around her waist, lifting her off her feet. She pulled her head back.

"You're the only man who has ever lifted me up," she said.

"Am I?"

"Yes. I've always felt…well, too big," she said. "I don't know why I'm telling you this. Must be the blindfold."

"Must be," he said, running his thumb down the side of her neck and slowly putting her back on her feet. "You're perfect, Jessie. I can only guess that other men didn't want you like I do."

"How's that?" she asked.

Honesty and fear caused the words to stick in his throat. He wanted her with a desperation that sometimes bordered on obsession. He thought about her night and day, and when she wasn't with him he wanted to be closer to her.

At the training center, sometimes he walked by her office to just to catch the lingering scent of her perfume.

She reached up, pushing the bandanna off, and their gazes met. She watched him the way she always did and he stood a little taller. Wanted to be the man he saw reflected in her eyes.

Then she looked toward the lights and her hand

went to her throat. She took a step back, her gaze moving over the picnic area and newly built fire, turning until she'd taken it all in.

"You did this for me?" she asked.

"Yes. I wanted to give you the stars," he said. "And this was as close as I could come to it."

That was more than he'd planned to admit, but it felt right. She felt right. She looked back at him.

"This is the most…just the most," she said.

"Thank you."

JESSIE HAD NEVER been given anything like this. Alexi, though he had loved her, was a practical man. He had been more inclined to buy her a new carabiner or a pair of trek shoes than to plan anything like this. It wasn't him.

And she'd thought for a long time that romance and these kinds of romantic evenings weren't her. But the butterflies in her stomach told a different story.

She couldn't stop looking around at the picnic area Hemi had prepared for them. It was perfect. Romantic, but not so over-the-top that she'd feel uncomfortable.

It was different, and that was kind of what made this evening and this man so special to her. He took her hand in his, brushing a kiss across the back of her knuckles.

"If my lady will allow, I'll help you take off your boots."

"Why do I need my boots off?" she asked.

"So you can walk over to the pillows…or I could carry you," he suggested.

She shook her head. "I'll take my boots off."

"Allow me," he said, going down on one knee. She rested her hands on his shoulders as she lifted her left foot toward him.

She felt silly, and at the same time a little bit sexy. His breath against her knee was warm. He pulled her boot off and set it aside, taking her foot in his hand to remove her thick sock.

"Not very sexy," she said.

"Everything about you is womanly, and that's a turn-on," he said.

He fingered the bandage around her ankle. "What happened?"

"Martinez tripped and I was trying to help him up and over a fallen log. I put a strain on my ankle."

Hemi bent and kissed her foot just below the bandage. "I'm sorry you were hurt."

She shrugged. "It's really nothing."

She'd had worse injuries swimming with jellyfish, but he was treating her…like she was fragile. It made her feel very feminine for the first time. Not, like she had always felt, too big to be a princess. Too big to be anything other than utilitarian. Someone who just got things done. He made her feel…delicate.

He helped her get her other boot off and then lifted her in his arms, like Rhett Butler carrying Scarlett O'Hara up the stairs.

"I thought I was going to walk over," she said.

"I decided I wanted to carry you," he replied.

Jessie did the only thing she could think of—she put her arm around his shoulder and rested her head against his neck as he carried her to the pillow nest. He set her down carefully and then went about pulling out their dinner dishes. Once their meal was served he sat down next to her.

"Alexi would never have done anything like this," she said, almost to herself.

"Tell me about him," Hemi said.

"You want to hear about my fiancé?"

He reached across the blanket and took her hand in his. "No. But I know that he's on your mind. I see glimpses of the past in your eyes and I want to understand that. He's a part of you, Jess. Maybe a part you think you lost, but he's still there."

She wiped her mouth with her napkin and then took her hand from his, wrapping her arms around her waist.

"What do you want to know?"

"What do you want to tell me?" he asked.

She tipped her head to the side, gave him a long level stare. "Alexi was brilliant about mountains. He could read the clouds and the way the sun fell on the snow. He just knew them as if he'd been born of them."

"He was Russian?"

"Yeah, but he'd grown up in the mountains of Afghanistan. He just liked to climb. We first met at a panel on extreme sporting. He was there talking about mountains, I was the ocean expert and we connected. We trained with each other in Colorado and then we'd go on our adventures. Sometimes together, most of the time not due to my filming schedule. Alexi had been reluctant to be on TV. When I got my television show I asked him to join me, but he said that he wasn't climbing for fame."

Hemi thought the guy sounded...like a saint. Like

a great man, and Hemi was sad that he'd never get to meet him. "How did you end up on Everest together?"

"We...truth?"

"Yes," he said.

She took a deep breath. "I think we both knew it was over. I really did enjoy the television stuff and the network wanted me to keep doing it. I was going to say yes, but it would keep me away from Alexi and I knew he disapproved. We went on the climb to see if our bond was still as strong as it had once been."

Hemi understood now why she was lost. He got it. "And he died."

"Yes. I...I keep thinking, well, a bunch of things, but I'm no closer to the truth," she said.

"I think Alexi must have been proud of you," Hemi said at last. "From what you've told me, he'd be mad that you're running from what you're meant to do."

She put her elbows next to her plate, leaning forward. "You think so?"

"I do. And I think, given enough time, you will, too."

Hemi was more romantic than she'd have guessed. She was seeing his true colors tonight and she was very much falling for him.

"I love this," she said. "You didn't have to do it, but I'm so glad you did."

"You're welcome," he said. "I wanted to tell you... well, what my world is like. Not necessarily what I see when I'm in space but what drew me to it. To my life."

She took a sip of her sparkling water. "What is it that made you obsessed with space?"

He put his plate aside and took hers, stacking

them before he leaned back, stretched out on the blanket and propped himself up on his elbow. "The stars. I used to walk down on the beach at night and look up at the sky and want to visit them all. I never thought… I never imagined that we'd advance enough that I'd be able to be as close to that fantasy as I am today. I thought maybe the moon, but being part of the path to Mars is something I never dared to dream of," he said.

"Yet here you are," she said.

"Most of the time I'm studying the area where the way station will be positioned, but I realized tonight is the peak of the Draconid meteor shower. Prime viewing time."

"What does that mean?"

"You'll see," he said, again. "If I describe it, I won't do it justice."

"Fair enough. What do I have to do?"

"Come over here and rest your head on my shoulder," he said.

She did as he asked. He wrapped his arm around her and held her closely to him as they watched the sky, and suddenly she saw it—a shooting star streaking across the sky, followed by another one and another.

She sat up, tipping her head back to get a better look at them. Hemi sat up and grabbed her hand. She squeezed his.

The piece of herself she'd lost when Alexi had slipped from her fingers into that crevasse was starting to come back. Sitting next to Hemi, listening to him talk about his passion, was giving her a fire in the pit of her belly to find hers again. To find her path, because a man of passion needed a woman who could match him.

Nothing could mar the beauty of this moment or this night. She knew that something was changing inside of her and it wasn't what she'd feared. She wasn't afraid of losing herself in Hemi. She was afraid she wouldn't be able to find herself in time to claim him and keep him.

She shoved those thoughts to the back of her mind and enjoyed this magical evening with her astronaut.

"THANKS FOR SHOWING me the meteor shower," Jessie said later, as they stood at her front door. "It reminded me of the bioluminescent organisms that my mom studies."

"You're welcome. I'd love to meet your folks," he said.

"Hemi…" she said.

"Yes?"

"We're not ready for that."

"I am."

"I'm not." She took a step back from him and reached behind her for the door handle. He was moving fast. But then, that was his way. "Thanks again for a nice evening. Good night."

"Good night."

_11_

JESSIE LED THE group of candidates away from the facility into the wilderness for a twenty-four-hour survival test. Since the night of the meteor shower last week they'd both been full-on with training. And Dennis had made it clear to her that she needed to focus on training, not late nights with the candidates. She was trying damned hard to make sure she was okay.

Hemi looked good to her. Leaner but stronger. She knew the intense regimen that all the astronauts participated in, and had seen him on the specialized treadmill when she passed the gym. But after the meteor shower, she was keeping her distance.

And she'd missed him.

So damned much.

She hadn't realized it until she found herself stealing glances at his chiseled jaw and remembering the feel of his lips on hers when they'd been out at that old homesteader's cabin. She'd run from him afterward, but now she'd give anything to have Hemi to herself. To know that they'd both always be under the stars together...

Hell.

Hemi had done the same thing. It was as if once they got close they both had to retreat. Both wanted to pretend that what had happened had meant nothing significant.

It was chilly on this October morning. It had been growing cooler and cooler as fall deepened its hold. She liked hiking in this kind of weather and if it were just a hike, she wondered if she'd be okay. Or more okay than she was in this moment. She knew the tests these candidates would have to face.

Jessie had taken one group through this test already and had been impressed by the way they had improvised. It was one of the things that Ace and Dennis always questioned her about. Were the candidates taking the lessons she'd prepared, the skills she was showing them, and adapting them for use in different circumstances? And the answer was a definite yes.

This group should be no different, except Hemi was in it. She hung toward the back once they got off the main path. Every member of this team had been given a different objective and Jessie was taking a backseat to watch how the candidates performed.

"Who drew the leader card?" Hemi asked.

"I did," Gregor Velosi said. He was in his mid-thirties and had been on several missions to the ISS. His call sign was Velocity, not just because of his name but also because he had accelerated through the ranks in the Air Force. He and Hemi had been on one mission together. As a payload specialist, he'd be in charge of operating the arm to assemble the main part of the way station. "Who has shelter?"

"Izzy and I," Jarvis said. "We will scout for a secure area and get to work building something."

"I'm on food," Hemi said. "I'll search for resources and then report back."

"Not on your own," Jessie said.

"No one else drew food," Hemi said. "Leo and Marcy are on resources."

"Can I have a word?" Jessie asked Hemi, gesturing for him to follow her. As soon as they were out of earshot of everyone else, she asked, "What's your deal?"

"Nothing. Just don't need you to be micromanaging me. I'm a leader and I know how to take care of my team."

"I wasn't challenging you. You can't just burst in and take over, everyone moves at a different pace."

"Everyone? Or you?"

She wrapped her arms around her waist. "Listen, this isn't about us. This is about the mission. You might be in charge of a team like this but you might have to take orders, too. You have to demonstrate you can do it. Otherwise…"

"Otherwise, I'm no good to my team," he said.

"Yes. It's not that your way isn't working, it's just that sometimes the slower path will be more successful for everyone involved."

"I was pushing you too hard," Hemi said.

She tipped her head to the side, studying him. She'd missed him this past week. Seeing him but never being alone with him, carefully making sure she wasn't caught staring at him…it had only heightened her awareness of him and made her want him more.

"You were. I get that it's your way of dealing with

things, but I'm used to planning, analyzing, planning some more, training, then reevaluating and taking action."

"I tried that. It makes me feel like I'm wearing a shirt that's too small. My arms are straining to wrap around you and tell you I can make things better. Just let me," Hemi said.

"You can't make it better. It's not that easy."

"I wish it were," he said. "Why can't you be—"

"Less me?" she asked.

"No. Never that. I don't think this would be as powerful if you weren't who you are. It's the fact that you don't need me to save you that appeals to me. You have to do it on your own and I get it. I do. But I also need you to need me."

And that was the one thing she didn't want to do.

He cursed under his breath and turned away from her. She let him go.

She had to.

The test was starting and he needed to be judged on it. A part of her knew that she was copping out. That she was using this test and the job to drive a wedge between them.

That didn't matter.

She needed to protect herself. She wasn't looking for a man to be a part of her life. She was trying to put the pieces of herself back together, and while sex with Hemi was out of this world, that was all she was willing to let it be.

HEMI PUSHED JESSIE out of his mind and for the next hour concentrated on the team. Though no one from the first group had revealed what took place on their overnight expedition, it didn't take a genius to figure out that they were going to be tested.

Thank God.

He needed to remind himself of something he was good at because he sure as shit wasn't getting it done with Jessie.

Every time he thought he had managed his own expectations, he came face-to-face with hers and realized he was lacking.

He wasn't used to a woman like her. He knew that. Hell, that was why he was so damned obsessed with her. And there were no two ways about it. He *was* obsessed.

He thought about her lips, how they felt under his. When they were apart, he thought her kiss couldn't taste as good as he remembered, and then he was kissing her and the taste was beyond what he remembered.

He existed in a permanent state of denial where she was concerned. He thought she couldn't be as beautiful as the picture he had of her his mind. Her long limbs, her full breasts and her heart-shaped face. And then he found himself staring at her as she walked into the clearing, noticing how long her neck was.

"Shelter and food, how are we coming on those?" she asked.

All business.

And damned if that didn't turn him on even more.

When she ignored him, he wanted her with a fierce thirst that he was beginning to think would never be quenched.

"I found some berries and I'm carrying rations for three days in my pack," Hemi spoke up.

"You are?" she asked.

"Yes. Never hurts to be prepared," he said.

"Hell, Thor, never pictured you as a Boy Scout," Velosi said.

"Did you picture me as dumb?" Hemi returned.

"Nah. I have two days' rations," Velosi admitted.

There were murmurs around the camp as others admitted they'd brought food, as well. It made sense and fit with the lessons they'd had with Jessie. In space they could only use what they brought with them.

"Good job," Jessie said. "Shelter? Where do we stand on that?"

The shelter team took Jessie aside to show her what they'd done. They'd made a rough lean-to that would house the entire team in the event of rain. Hemi looked around the area and noticed some holes in the ground.

"What are those?" he asked Izzy, who was closest to him.

She peered at the ground and then took a step closer to him. "Those look like moccasin nests. We have them in northern Texas. Is there a water source around here?"

"The lake, Bombshell," Jarvis said. "Don't you remember seeing it on the way out? Why are you asking?"

"I think that might be a snake nest," Izzy said.

"Do you know how to deal with them?"

"To be honest, in North Texas we fill the holes in and then get the hell away from them."

Hemi waited to see if Velosi would give the order but the other man was silent. Hemi shook his head.

"You two, fill in the holes and the rest of you gather up our supplies. Let's find a better location for our base camp," Hemi said.

He took over directing the team away from the danger and noticed that Jessie stood back observing. Part of him knew that was what she was supposed to do, but another part of him realized it was her way. She kept herself back from him and from everyone.

Even on the Bar T she didn't socialize with the others, preferring to keep to herself. He knew that it was important, maybe even the key to trying to make this relationship between them work, but he tucked the fact away for later. Saving his team from danger was priority number one.

When the holes were filled in, he directed the rest of the team to join the others and Jessie followed them. He reached out to grab her wrist and stop her.

"Did you know about the snakes?" he asked.

She bit her lip. She had a little bit of dirt on her cheek from where she'd wiped her hand on her face. He reached out and brushed it off. "Yes."

"That was a big risk," he said.

"Ace suggested it. He said if something went wrong in space someone could die. I have antivenin in my bag and we have emergency staff at the barn on the Bar T. Dennis and Ace need to know who they are sending on this mission," Jessie said. "This isn't like Everest where it's just me against the mountain… You have to be able to depend on your team, Hemi. And I want to make sure that you have the best around you."

"Why?" he asked. He understood, but he wanted to hear her say it.

She shook her head, tugged her wrist from his hand. "You matter to me. I know your nickname is Thor, but I thought there was more to you than muscles and good times."

She walked away and he watched her leave.

But somehow he felt closer to her than he had before. He followed her and the rest of the team, distracted by the thought that he couldn't wait to get her alone and explore her response further.

A few hours later found them all sitting around a fire, telling tales about how they'd come to be astronauts. How the evening sky and the infinite promise of the cosmos had drawn them from their homes and shaped their dreams. All the while, Hemi had to admit that he was thinking about Jessie.

JESSIE LISTENED TO the stories and had one of those déjà vu moments. She'd heard the same passion millions of times in the voices of sailors and marine biologists from the Galapagos to Monterey Bay when they spoke of the sea, and from Sherpas in the Himalayas talking about the mountains with the same reverence. The same longing.

"Tell us about Everest," Izzy said. "I always thought a person had be crazy to pit themselves against the elements like that."

Jessie leaned back on her elbow and glanced over at the other woman. "Crazy is going into space. There's no Sherpa at your back or base camp safety for your retreat."

"At least we have a spaceship or station around

us up there. When you're on Everest, what do you have?" Hemi asked.

"Sheer will and determination. That feeling like you can do anything you want," she said.

"It's like that for me when I'm buckled in waiting for liftoff, and then it's like I'm riding an enormous wave," Velosi said. "My wife said I had to be crazy but it's not crazy…"

"No, it's not," Izzy said. "It's like knowing you are where you are meant to be."

"Exactly," Jessie said. Realizing how much she had in common with these people who were so very different from herself was humbling.

"What made you come here?" Velosi asked. "I can't imagine anything making me walk away from NASA."

Alexi's face flashed in her mind's eye, and for the first time in months, she felt the comfort she had always felt around him instead of that crushing guilt. Time and her own slow acceptance were giving her the buffer she needed to think of him without the pain of his death. "I had a scare the last time I was up there. The weather and the loss of a dear friend made me…well, just made me think I needed to take some time away from the mountains. Try another adventure."

There were nods and murmurs around the campfire.

"I'm glad you're here," Izzy said. "I've learned a lot from your lessons. I thought…well, that they might be a waste of time, but there is so much I hadn't considered when it comes to survival."

One of the other women, Marcy, said, "That first

day, when we immediately had to use what you'd told us about the cold…that was powerful. Made me realize maybe I was relying too much on the environmental systems on the space station."

As the evening progressed, talk turned to stories of near misses, and Jessie realized that despite the fact that they were all competing for a slot on the first mission, there was a feeling of camaraderie between them. They were a fraternity, and they all wanted to see each other succeed.

It was something she'd never really wanted for herself. She thought perhaps it was down to her solitary childhood, but she'd always been more interested in proving to herself she could do it.

"You okay?" Hemi asked, coming over and sitting down next to her.

She looked up into his face and realized how much he'd changed her. She had been afraid of losing herself, and a part of her, if she were being completely honest, felt like she had.

"Yeah," she said, limiting herself to that one-word reply, because she was afraid if she kept talking she'd say too much. Reveal what was in the hidden chaos of her mind. The fact that Hemi Barrett, with his square jaw, rugged good looks and Maori birthmark had changed something fundamental inside of her. He'd made her look at the world in a way that she hadn't expected to.

And that was precisely why she'd taken this job. To change. To get out of her own mind and find the path back to living and not just existing. But she hadn't counted on Hemi.

Hadn't counted on how he made her feel and the

fact that she felt too much for him. It was jumbled and confused but she couldn't deny the feelings she had for him.

"What are you thinking?" he asked.

"Something that I can't say here. You should bunk down with the others," she said.

"I don't want to."

"Hemi."

"Jessie."

"Damn, you're the most stubborn man I've met," she said. He pushed her and not exactly in a subtle way.

"Good. You need someone who stands in your way. Keeps you on your toes," he said. "Are you pushing me away because of work—the test? Or because you don't want anyone to see us together?"

She shrugged. She couldn't be caught between her lover and her job.

"Please just go bunk down," she said. "I need you to do this for me."

"Fair enough. But when we get back I have two days' leave that I want to take. Will you come away with me?" he asked.

She could ask for time off. She was supposed to write up evaluations of all the candidates, but then she was free while they concentrated on learning the ins and outs of the way station they'd be building between Earth and Mars.

"Yes."

"No takesies-backsies," he said.

"I'm not wishy-washy, Hemi. I want some time away from here with you so that maybe I can gain some perspective on what is going on."

"Good," he said, getting up and walking over to the others. She sat there by the dying embers of the fire, staring into the heart of it and seeing not this night but the future. Though it was still hazy, she finally had an idea of where she wanted to go.

12

JESSIE HAD BEEN in meetings all day and hadn't seen the sun since 6 a.m. She stretched as she walked down the hall and closed her eyes. She was sure she could smell Hemi's aftershave.

She shook her head to try to get him out of it but it didn't work. It was late at night and almost all of the trainees were in their quarters for the night. She was alone in this part of the facility, having stayed late to finish writing up her assessments.

She had worn a pair of cargo pants to work and a button-down flannel shirt over her NASA golf shirt that Hemi had told her made her blue eyes even bluer.

She shook her head.

Really, when had she become that kind of woman? The kind who perked up when a man complimented her? But she knew it wasn't any man who had that power over her, just Hemi.

He'd been wearing a pair of jeans this morning with a big leather belt and an Oxford-style shirt with the Cronus mission logo on the left breast. He'd looked professional and sexy.

He'd wanted to get away with her, but his leave had been canceled. One of the astronauts on the ISS, a British national, had been doing some remote testing of the Mars Rover from orbit around the Earth. His trial had been successful, and Dennis and Ace wanted to test their team. So a new simulation had been written and now all of the candidates were working on building the way station remotely.

She was fascinated by the changes that happened every day with the space program and especially the Cronus missions.

But she did miss Hemi. She had been looking forward to being away from the Bar T and their lives here.

Sometimes she was taken aback by how much her daily routine had become dependent on seeing him. He wasn't always in her classes, so there were weeks when she only saw him once or twice. Probably why she thought she'd caught a whiff of his aftershave.

Wishful dreaming, that was what her father called it.

She heard the low rumble of Hemi's voice around the corner and quickened her steps, wishing she didn't feel like...like a woman who cared deeply for a man. She hadn't felt this way in a long time. She and Alexi had been together for what felt like an eternity and the first blush of falling for each other had faded. At times she'd felt that they were an old married couple, happily going about their routines.

She hugged that memory close and stopped walking to lean against the cold cement wall of the hallway. Hemi wasn't going to be the suburban husband/dad. Not that her dream scenario was one of suburban living, but he was always going to be away from her more than he was with her.

She knew how these astronauts thought. She'd learned over the months she'd been at the Mick Tanner Training Facility how important it was to each of them to be either on a mission or training for one.

None of them wanted to be grounded.

They were all very aware of each thing they ate, the exercises they did and how it impacted their chances of participating in the program.

None more than Hemi.

He was made to lead. She suspected he would be chosen to head future missions. She knew from discussions with Molly and Ace that Ace didn't plan to go on more than one mission to the Cronus way station. He wanted to lead that mission and then come back here and settle down with Molly.

Training others to go to Mars and possibly farther.

Hemi was standing there as she rounded the corner, his head resting back against the wall, one hand at his waist the other hanging loosely by his side, holding a bottle of water.

She cleared her throat and he turned his head without lifting it from the wall. He gave her a long, level look from under his thick eyelashes.

"Jessie."

It was just her name, but it sounded like an invitation. She walked over until only a few inches separated them. He put his hand out, catching her waist and drawing her closer to him. He wrapped his arms around her, burying his head in her neck and she felt the heavy beat of his heart through the thin layers of their clothes.

His breath was hot against her skin and a shudder of awareness went through her. She could tell that he was upset. Something had happened. But her body's needs were more urgent. She needed him. Instead of weeks, it felt like it had been months since she'd had him inside of her.

She'd never thought of herself as a sexual being, but around Hemi it seemed she was. She rubbed her hands up and down his big broad back, then reached behind him to cup his ass and hold him to her.

"What's the matter?" she asked.

He sighed again, squeezing her waist and then lifting his head to stare down at her. In his dark eyes she saw so much but understood too little. There was no mistaking that he was going through something emotional but she really couldn't put her finger on what it was.

"Talk to me," she said.

"I will."

His voice was low and gravelly. It rubbed over her already aroused senses and she shivered.

She went on tiptoe, still holding his butt. She took his bottom lip between her teeth and tugged at it before kissing him. She took his mouth the way she wanted to take him. With no inhibitions and no thought to the consequences.

His hips jerked forward and she felt the ridge of his cock between them. Felt him rub himself against her and she arched herself into him.

He felt good.

For the life of her she couldn't remember why she'd been so adamant that she should keep her distance from him.

She needed him and this.

She took his hand and led him down the hall to her office. She used the fingerprint sensor to open the door and drew him in behind her. The door closed and she turned, putting her hand in the middle of Hemi's chest, pushing him back against the solid door.

He arched one eyebrow at her.

"Is this my one-on-one?"

"Yes."

She untucked his shirt and he lifted his arms over his head, drawing it off. She stepped back to admire him. He was all muscles. She reached out to trace his tattoo, leaning in closer to use her tongue to follow the pattern until it disappeared into his waistband. With the tip of her fingernail she traced the line between his skin and the cloth, slipping her finger underneath.

He groaned, raising her head so he could bring his mouth down hard on her. She sucked his tongue deep into her mouth and felt everything feminine in her awaken.

"Jessie, babe. I need you," he said.

His cock pushed against the fabric of his pants but she knew that he wanted more from her than just sex. He needed something from her that she wanted to give him.

Solace.

A chance to escape whatever was on his mind. It was what she needed, too. Something big had happened today at NASA. She didn't know what it was, but everyone had been tense walking up and down the halls.

Tonight he was hers. For a few hours she could be

with Hemi and not think about the future or even the present. Not worry that she'd lost herself forever and that this might be all she could claim of him.

She undid his belt, unbuttoned his pants and slowly lowered the zipper until she could push her hand into the opening. She stroked her hand up and down the length of his cock. He wore plain cotton boxer briefs. She rubbed her finger over the tip as she dropped nibbling kisses all along his abdomen. She shoved his pants down. He put his hands under her arms and lifted her to her feet. Setting her to one side, he toed off his shoes and then stepped out of the clothes.

He was naked, his sex jutting out proudly.

In her office.

Hers.

She took her time running her hands over his body. She loved the muscled strength of him, the hard ridges of his abs leading down to his tattoo. She bent and traced it again, let her tongue follow the edge of the scroll that formed its border and then moved her way around his back. She used her hands to push him.

"What are you doing?"

"I want to see all of you. Usually…"

"Usually?"

"You're in charge and I'm so wrapped up in what's going on with me and how you make me feel that I haven't been able to explore you."

"Wouldn't you rather do this in a bed?" he asked.

"Yes, but I don't want to wait. I want you now."

"I want you, too," he said, tangling his hands in her hair. "I need you, Jess."

"I need you, too," she said.

She'd been thinking about him all day long. She didn't know what her deal was. In the past she'd thought about sex maybe once or twice in a year, but with Hemi she thought about it all the time.

"I want to do this."

"Okay, but I want you naked," he said.

She nodded, kicking her shoes off as he undid the buttons of her flannel shirt and pushed it off her shoulders. She shrugged out of her golf shirt and Hemi stopped helping her, playing with her breasts instead. She wore a demi bra with lace cups, and he pushed the lace down until he could touch her nipples.

She closed her eyes for a second, enjoying the feel of his hands on her until she remembered *she* was seducing *him*. She reached behind her back and undid her bra, letting it fall free as she undressed.

She stood there in front of him, naked. His cock jerked as he skimmed his gaze over her and she stood a little taller, proud that he wanted her body. That looking at her could turn him on as much it had.

Unable to wait any longer, she closed the gap between them, her hand going for his cock again.

He was warm and hard, and she liked the way he felt as she moved her hand up and down his length.

"Woman."

"Yes?" she asked, swiping her finger over his tip.

She bent down, taking the crown of it into her mouth. He groaned her name and tried to pull her head back. She looked up and their eyes met. He groaned, tangled his hands in her hair and urged her forward after all. She licked his shaft. She liked the taste of him, and the musky smell that she associated only with Hemi.

She took him into her mouth again. He thrust his cock deep and she swallowed around him. Sucked him deeper. She swirled her tongue around the head of his cock as she clenched his buttocks, holding him to her.

He pulled her head back. "Enough."

She started to protest but he drew her to her feet. He spun her around and slid his hand between her legs, his fingers thrusting deep into her body. Her head fell backward against his shoulder and she couldn't think. Could only feel the thickness of him as he rubbed himself between her buttocks. His fingers were driving her toward orgasm as he put his hand under her jaw and drew her head back to kiss her neck.

She shivered and shuddered in his arms as he continued to work her with his fingers. She was on the edge, close to an orgasm, but she couldn't come. She reached up and took her nipple between her fingers to pinch it.

He brought his free hand up, his nail scraping around her belly button then rising until he put his hand over hers and used her hand to massage her breast. He squeezed it tight and then rotated her palm over her nipple until it was pointed and hard. Then he moved his hand off of hers and cupped her other breast. He plucked her nipple between his thumb and forefinger as she continued to rock back and forth against his hand.

He held her prisoner of her own desire. His hands were on her and in her and she desperately needed more. She turned her head and found his mouth, bit down on his bottom lip as he flicked her clit with his thumb before plunging his fingers deeper into her body.

Her orgasm rocked through her, her flesh shuddering and shaking as he continued to play with her, letting her ride his fingers until her orgasm passed. She turned in his arms, lifting her leg to wrap around his waist, and reached between them, taking the long length of him in her hands and positioning him at her center. She looked up at him and he smiled.

She rubbed her finger over the mark around his right eye and felt her heart clench. She loved him.

The knowledge rolled through her as surely as her climax just had. He took her wrist in one hand, stretching her arm up over her head as he held her hip with his other hand and drove into her. She felt as though he went so deep they'd be connected forever.

She knew her heart was already tied to him and she wrapped her other thigh around his hips, trusting him to support her, and, being Hemi, he did. He drove into her deeply, but slowly.

Their passion built with each thrust of his lean hips. She let her head fall backward and watched him through narrowed eyes. He brought his mouth down on hers and kissed her deeply. His tongue matched the rhythm of his hips until she started suckling on it.

He pounded into her again and again, driving her up and up, and her walls clenched around him. She watched him through narrowed eyes as he continued pounding into her until she threw her head back, crying out his name as she came.

She reached between their bodies, past his thrusting hips, found his balls and squeezed them lightly. He jerked and she felt him curse as he jetted into her. He filled her completely before leaning heavily against her, his mouth on her breast, his breath brushing over her midriff.

She held him to her, surprised that her limbs had any strength left in them. He'd taken everything she had, pulled it from her, and as she slowly came back into herself, she finally understood that she was never going to be the same again.

She was never going to be anything other than this new woman who was Hemi's. This new woman who saw the path of her life spreading out in a direction she'd never anticipated.

She had no one but herself to blame. All her life she'd spent time in nature with safe men like Alexi, men who were similar to her. Maybe a part of her had understood that if she ever gave herself to a man like Hemi, she'd no longer own herself. She'd never want to step off the path they could travel together.

He lifted her and turned, sinking down on the floor. He cradled her, letting her rest her head on his shoulder and running his fingers through her hair. She closed her eyes.

Fear and love were twin emotions roiling through her, but love was stronger.

And scarier. Just because she felt like this didn't mean Hemi would want her as deeply as she did him.

Loving him and letting him go to space was going to be hard, but loving him and having him not love her back would be devastating, something she'd never recover from.

He held her tightly and finally lifted his head; the look in his dark eyes scared her a little bit.

"Can I take you home?" he asked. "I want to spend the night wrapped in your arms."

She nodded.

They dressed quickly and linked hands as they walked out of the facility. She'd been careful not to let anyone know they were dating, but whatever had happened today had changed that.

She hugged his arm to her body, and when they got to her cabin they went straight to her bedroom.

He took her clothes off carefully and then made tender love to her. She fell asleep in his arms.

13

THE CABIN JESSIE had been given was slowly coming to feel like home to her. It was odd, because she'd never thought of a place as home before. The floor was covered with rugs she'd had in storage that she'd purchased over the years. A hammered metal bowl that had been a gift to her from a Hindu priest in India graced her living room table. A native Lapland woven blanket hung on the wall above the fireplace. And she'd strung prayer flags she'd gotten in the Himalayas across the doorway leading into the kitchen.

This place was slowly becoming hers.

She had a picture she'd snapped of Hemi when they'd walked to the lake so he could show her the orbit of a satellite he was in charge of monitoring. He was backlit by the setting sun and he'd looked at her...well, like no man had before.

He'd grabbed her phone out of her hand and snapped a few selfies of the two of them. She'd used a filter on the photos and then printed them out with her color printer.

She hoped to pick up a frame in town when she went shopping with Molly soon.

She reached out and touched the photo of her own personal Thor.

She usually thought of him as Hemi and not Thor. At first, she'd thought of him as two distinctly different men—the astronaut and her lover. But she didn't do that anymore. She accepted him as he was. All of him.

Which wouldn't be a problem if she wasn't starting to think of this place on the Bar T ranch in Cole's Hill, Texas, as her home. And she pictured her home with Hemi by her side.

After a lifetime of wandering, taking on nature and never letting a challenge go unmet, it was odd to her that she wasn't craving the next adventure.

Instead, she had downloaded a recipe off the internet that Molly had Pinned…oh, heavens, she was addicted to Pinterest. It didn't matter, she liked it. It was nice to go to sleep without feeling her heartbeat in the blisters on her feet. And while she was still active, her muscles didn't ache at night.

She had invited Molly, Izzy and a few other women over for dinner and drinks this evening. Dinner and drinks. She liked it.

She liked this new woman she was becoming and that scared her. This new life she was embarking on had an anchor at the center of it.

Hemi.

She hadn't counted on that. She'd tried to be careful not let herself care too deeply for him, but that ship had sailed. There was something about him that spoke to her body, mind and soul. She dreamed of him and when he could spend the night next to her in bed.

Those were both the best and worst nights. How could she deny that she wanted him with her? She wanted Hemi in her life forever. She wanted him to stay here with her and train astronauts, not go on a mission that would take him halfway to Mars.

She also knew that she'd never ask him to be less than himself. And for Hemi there was only the life up there in the stars.

She walked away from the photo grouping and over to her desk. She rubbed the back of her neck as she sat down.

She had the power to keep Hemi here with her.

She had been asked to rate and review every astronaut. She could say he wasn't ready or that his skills weren't up to par, but this was Hemi Barrett. Even if she was so desperate to try to ground him, she wouldn't do it—she *couldn't*.

She knew what it was like to be called to do something that few others understood. How could she live with herself if she did something to sabotage him?

She put her head in her hands, her elbows on her desk. She closed her eyes and inhaled the fragrance of the sea from a candle Hemi had given her. He'd included a note, saying he knew she missed the ocean.

And she did, but not the way she would miss him.

It touched her that he knew this about her. That he'd been watching her, observing her closely and had picked up on it.

She wanted to return the favor.

Her friend who was an expert on Maori tribal art had emailed her, but she hadn't wanted to download the message and images to her phone because the memory on her phone wasn't great and she always had a problem when she tried to download to it.

She lifted her head. *Purpose.* She had something she needed to do.

She opened her email and carefully read the description of the tribal art that was associated with Hemi's family tattoo. It came as no surprise to her that they were descendants of an ancient family. Legend said the elaborate scroll in the middle of his ink marked him as a descendant of the gods. Which was fitting.

She also read that the other marks represented strength—not physical strength, but more like integrity, honor and loyalty.

These symbols were all things she already associated with Hemi and she wasn't surprised that his family's ink denoted it.

His crest, if he'd been of European descent, would have had the same marks.

She felt ashamed that she'd even thought of trying to keep him from space. A man such as Hemi deserved a woman who could fight by his side. Stand by him whenever he needed. Smile and let him go off on an eighteen-month mission and never let him know that when he did, he'd take a piece of her heart with him.

COLE'S HILL WAS one of those medium-sized towns that had seen a boom during its oil days and, thanks to its proximity to Houston, had blossomed. It was full of trendy boutiques and upscale restaurants.

They had a thriving ranch industry, but also a decent tourist trade.

Molly remembered the town from her youth, when it was smaller and more rural. She said she used to know just about everyone.

"This is why I don't like coming to town," Molly said, as she led the way to Old Bones Microbrewery.

"Seems like you're the one everyone wants to talk to," Jessie said.

"Yeah. It's only because of the training facility. I didn't anticipate that when we decided to bid on the NASA project to save the ranch," Molly said.

"I wouldn't have anticipated it, either," Jessie said.

"Girl, how you talk," Molly said with a wink. "Take that booth in the corner and I'll grab us some drinks. This place is one of the best microbreweries in Texas…and that's saying something."

Jessie laughed. Molly was a proud Texan. Though Jessie had heard her friend complain about the heat in the dead of summer, she still was Texan through and through.

Jessie slid onto the solid wood bench. It was cold on the backs of her thighs. She and Molly had gone shopping and Jessie had bought two dresses, a miniskirt and a pair of hand-tooled Western boots.

And Jessie, who'd never really spent any time shopping in a women's boutique before, had been satisfied with her purchases. She wore the denim miniskirt now with her Irish wool sweater and her new boots. It was late fall, so the air was nippy but not cold.

Her phone beeped and she had to scramble to find it. That was one thing about being back in the civilized world that she was still adjusting to. Her phone was her lifeline to everyone else at the facility. When she was on her adventures in extremely remote parts of the world, she'd only pull out her high-tech satellite phone for a real emergency.

She unlocked the phone and shook her head when she saw the message was from Molly.

The bartender recognized you and wants to take a selfie with you. I told him you liked your privacy... unless you want to?

Jessie had grown up on television and she'd been able to do anything she chose her entire life, so refusing a photograph with a fan wasn't something she felt she should do.

Jessie slid out of the booth and walked over to the bar.

"Hi, I'm Jessie," she said, holding her hand out to the bartender.

"Travis, but everyone calls me Trav."

"It's nice to meet you, Trav. Want me to come around the bar and Molly can snap a photo of us?"

"That would be great. My brother is going to be so jealous. We used to spend hours pretending to be on the *Calypso*, on an adventure like your family."

"I'd love to hear about those adventures."

"Well, they mostly involved us jumping and climbing on stuff. Mom wasn't too pleased with that," Trav said.

They continued to talk about her adventures with her parents and how Trav and his brother had started their bar/microbrewery, and then Molly took a photo of them and the women headed back to their table.

"That was really sweet of you," Molly said after she took a sip of her beer.

"You think? I never mind talking to fans. So many people watched our show. Mom said we were blessed," Jessie said. So lucky, her parents had told her. They lived a life they loved because of the television show.

"I forget you're famous," Molly said.

"Well, I'm not like Hemi or Ace," Jessie said.

"I know. Can't come to town with those guys or everyone wants a minute of their time."

"I think it's cool," Jessie said. "I was flattered when they asked me to be on the training team."

"I know what you mean. I'm still pinching myself that I'm part of the facility."

Their food was delivered. Molly had ordered a large burger with bacon and cheese, and Jessie, diet-conscious for too long, had ordered a veggie patty. Though, when she saw Molly's plate, she was tempted to send her veggie burger back.

Molly laughed as she noticed Jessie staring at her plate.

"Want half?"

"Yes." Jessie didn't even hesitate.

Molly cut her burger in two and handed one piece to Jessie. "Is that why you asked me to come into town with you? Because Ace gets mobbed?"

"Nope. I'm pissed at Ace."

"Why? Is the wedding off?"

"No. But he's been sleeping alone."

"What's going on?"

"The mission has been pushed back by three months."

"I didn't know that," Jessie said. No wonder Hemi had seemed preoccupied. But that meant he would be with her longer than she'd anticipated.

"I found out in an email from Dennis. Not from my fiancé, who you think would share something important like that."

"Did he say why he didn't?"

"He didn't want to worry me…that's what he said. Then I was like, why would I worry?" Molly took another bite of her burger.

"Why would you?"

"Because they are taking an experimental rocket up into space. It's going to be the test launch and no one has done any of this before," Molly said.

"Isn't that true of most of the Cronus mission program?" Jessie asked.

"My point. To which he replied that he thought I'd seen the email that showed the rocket burning up on reentry. They don't know how to get them back with this new technology," Molly said. "They will keep testing until they get it right, but it just brought home how dangerous this mission could be. Why can't he just be a cowboy, you know?"

Jessie put her burger down as her stomach churned. She'd thought she was aware of the dangers that Hemi faced, but she hadn't been. She couldn't prepare him to survive that.

Molly took a deep swallow of her beer. "I thought

the worst thing would be missing him for eighteen months, but that he might not come back..."

Jessie reached for her friend's hand and clung tightly to it.

HEMI KNOCKED ON her door and then shifted back on his heels. He should be in the gym doing another hour on the RED machine but instead he was here.

He'd seen the Facebook post from the Old Bones Microbrewery. Seen that photo of her smiling with some guy. And all he'd been able to think was...

Mine.

Jessie was his. He didn't want her taking photos with young guys who owned local businesses. A guy who'd be just up the road from her while he was in space doing his job. A guy who could probably give her something that Hemi couldn't—an easygoing relationship.

That guy—Trav, the Facebook post had said—wouldn't push Jessie's boundaries.

The first time Hemi had met her, something had passed between the two of them and it hadn't weakened over time. Instead, the last month had simply strengthened his desire for her.

Made him want her and need her in his life even more than he had before.

He wasn't going to front and pretend she was just a casual playmate. He'd had women like that before, but Jessie was different.

When they were apart all he could do was think about her. Every time he walked past her damned office he got a hard-on remembering the way she'd taken him there and made him...

Hell, made him realize there was no letting her go.

Jessie had carved a spot for herself in his soul and no matter how far he went into the universe, he would always carry her with him.

He knew it.

And it was about damned time she knew it, as well.

The door to her cabin opened when he knocked and he saw her standing there. Her blond hair hung around her face, framing her high cheekbones. Her legs were bare and long. He remembered vividly the last time they'd been wrapped around him.

Her feet, those long, lovely feet, were bare and her toenails were painted a pumpkin-y shade of orange.

He skimmed his gaze back up her body as he reached for her waist to pull her toward him but she wedged her hand between them.

"What's wrong?" he asked.

"Molly told me about the rocket test," she said. Her anger wasn't fiery like his was, but cold. Icy. He knew she upset. He didn't blame her. He wasn't too thrilled himself.

She turned and walked into the house, leaving the door open.

He followed her, but there was a lump that felt like lead in his stomach. He closed the door behind him and looked around. Her place was warm and welcoming. She'd made this cabin her own. Just as he'd made her his own—but he'd tried to ignore the cost to her when he left, or the dangers that he would face.

He couldn't walk away for her or NASA. He wouldn't.

But he didn't want to hurt her.

He hadn't told anyone about the rocket test failure. A part of him was afraid that if he started talking about it, the reality of the dangers of going into space—the part he always ignored when he was in the Johnson Space Center and walked past the plaques honoring the astronauts who'd died—would be too real.

"I don't think Molly was supposed to share that," Hemi said, because he didn't want to face her with the truth. He was scared to. Not enough to stop training or to recuse himself from the running. But he was afraid.

Jessie stopped walking, pivoting on her heel to face him.

Fuck.

He knew what a Valkyrie looked like now. He saw it in the lines of her tall body and her blazing, ice-blue eyes. He saw the strength and the courage and the anger in her.

He cursed inwardly as he realized that he was buoyed by her strength. It just made him care for her that much more.

He knew he was on shaky ground here. He had to handle this the right way or he wasn't going to be welcome here again.

But he couldn't think.

There weren't words that were going to reassure her because he had none to reassure himself.

"Are you fucking kidding me?" she asked.

He shrugged, unsure how to talk about it. The fear. For himself and for her.

"Molly told me because she needed someone to

talk about this with. Why didn't you tell me?" she asked.

She paced toward him, three long strides that made the hem of her skirt rise on her thighs. He watched her, his blood racing and emotions rising up in him like a storm.

One he couldn't control.

He reached for her, and this time when she ducked out of his grasp he was ready for her. He caught her, wrapped both arms around her and held her tightly.

Her response was to punch him with her free hand, hard in the shoulder. He loosened his grip on her and looked down into her eyes.

They were watery, sad and mad at the same time.

"I'm scared, too," he said, his voice low and guttural. Raw.

She stopped struggling, wrapped her arms around him and held him tightly.

He rocked her back and forth but solace wasn't going to be found in this.

So he lifted her off her feet and carried her down the hall into her bedroom.

He reached under her skirt and tore her panties off while she undid his jeans. They came together hot and hard, neither having the time for a slow seduction. He wanted to make it gentle, to try to find a way to tell her with his body all the things he couldn't find the words to say, but he couldn't.

He just wanted to take her, thrust into her again and again until she was marked as his. Until he knew she'd never forget him, no matter what happened when he went on his Cronus mission.

14

JESSIE ROLLED ONTO her side when Hemi got up from the bed and went into the bathroom. She heard the sound of the taps, but she couldn't move. She felt raw and scared. Like all the growth she'd had, all the discoveries she'd made, had left her and she was back where she'd been when she first arrived in Texas.

She remembered their morning horseback ride and how she'd had that flash of him slipping into the crevasse instead of Alexi and mixed them together. Her subconscious was telling her that there was no safety net. There were no guarantees in love.

She hadn't realized that until this moment.

Hemi came back into the room. He was so big and strong that it was almost inconceivable that anything could happen to him. He lifted her up without saying a word and carried her into the bathroom. He'd run a bath and he set her on her feet next to the tub.

The tub was a normal one, not big or fancy, but it was filled with warm water and a layer of bubbles. He'd lit the candles she had on the counter next to the sink. She knew he was trying. Her heart, so battered by emotions she was struggling to contain and couldn't yet catalog, beat a little faster.

"Want to have a bath with me?" he asked.

Now he was gentle. And it was in the gentleness that she saw his fear. Saw the words he was afraid to say. She nodded. He held his hand out to her and she took it for balance as she climbed into the tub. She went toward the end without the taps but he held her still.

"Wait."

He climbed in and sat, then drew her down between his legs. The water sloshed a little over the sides as they settled and she leaned back against his chest. He didn't say anything, just held her with one arm while he ran his other hand over her body.

"I'm sorry I didn't say anything about the rocket," he said, his voice rusty, as if he hardly used it. "I've been trying to figure out a way to tell you for days but I didn't want to admit that even now, in the twenty-first century, we can still lose equipment and…dammit, people. We were lucky the rocket was just a test. The timeline is crucial."

She put her hand on his arm around her waist and squeezed it. "I've been training you all to survive extreme situations, thinking of a malfunction in space where it would take weeks or months for rescuers to get to you, but it never even occurred to me that the real danger could be much closer to home."

He tipped her head back on his shoulder so that their eyes met.

"I'm sorry."

"I believe you," she said. How could she tell him that she wasn't sure she could continue on with him?

That she didn't want to lose another lover. What was wrong with her that she was drawn to these men who could do incredible things but who also took great risks?

Even as she had the thought, tears burned her eyes and she tried to turn away, but Hemi held her jaw, refusing to let her.

"What is it?"

"I don't want to lose you," she said. Her voice was guttural and raw, and she hated that. The tracks of her tears were hot, and Hemi cursed as he lifted her up, turning her so she straddled his hips.

"I don't want to lose you, either," he said, framing her face and using his big thumbs to wipe away her tears. "I'm not planning on letting you go."

She put her hands on his shoulders and leaned until their foreheads rested against each other. She closed her eyes, because up close his dark gaze seemed like an endless abyss—one she could easily lose herself in.

"Jessie?"

She shook her head, then took deep breaths to try to get control. Since the moment Molly had told her about the explosion she'd been on a knife's edge. She felt like she was back on Everest, making a climb in the worst conditions and feeling, not Alexi this time, but Hemi behind her. Knowing that if she took the wrong step it would put him at risk.

It was something she didn't want to face.

"Jessie. Look at me," he said.

She opened her eyes and shifted back. "What?"

"It was a test. It was a failure, but they will fix it.

NASA and many other space agencies have invested too much to let this mission fail."

"I know," she said. She did know that. They would do something different and try again. And eventually Hemi would be strapped into a seat and blasted into space and she'd have no control over what happened to him.

She remembered the saying, the one about loving someone and letting them go, and for the first time in her life she got it. She loved him. And being an astronaut, and the risks associated with it, was very much a part of who Hemi was. She just had to let him do what he was called to do.

She wanted to. She wanted to love him enough to be unselfish but she was afraid that she couldn't. She wouldn't let him know, though. Not now.

So she nodded, took the loofah from where she kept it on the edge of the tub and started washing his chest. In her mind she weighed her options. And knew that the truth was going to come down to whether she could love him enough to do what was right for him and not for herself.

"I'm just glad you're here with me tonight," she said.

"Me, too."

SOMETHING MADE HIM feel edgy. Something about Jessie. It was bad enough dealing with his own fear. But this thing with Jessie. Something had changed.

He knew it.

He saw it. Not in the tears that she'd cried but in the way she was washing him. Her hands moved slowly over her him as if she were memorizing his body. His heart skipped a beat and a lump as solid as moon rock settled in his stomach. She was going to say goodbye.

He wasn't ready.

And then it hit him that even though he'd thought he understood what it meant to find the love of his life, until just now, sitting in the bathtub with Jessie naked on his lap, he hadn't gotten it. He needed her.

He wrapped his arms around her and held her to him. She had sharpened everything in his life. She was wrapped around his heart and he'd made a place for her deep in his soul. He hoped she'd done the same for him. It felt like they were intertwined.

"Jessie—"

"Did I tell you my friend finally got back to me about the origin of your tattoo?" she asked, shifting further down his thighs and reaching out with her free hand to touch the symbols and scrolls.

He wanted that information, but he saw she was trying to avoid what he needed to say.

"No, you didn't. You can tell me about it later," he said. "I want to—"

She put her fingers over his mouth. They were wet and sudsy, and she looked up at him with wide, wounded eyes. He realized she couldn't talk now. He wanted to force the issue, to force her to talk this out, but he knew if he did, this would be the last time they would be together. She was on the verge of breaking and needed time to recover.

He should let her.

But he didn't want to let her rebuild her walls. He wanted to pull her into the shelter of his body and promise that he'd keep her safe.

But how could he?

He didn't know the future. He didn't know if he would be here when she needed him. He wanted to be, but that wasn't the same thing.

"Tell me about it," he said at last.

She nodded and her let her hand fall again to his tattoo. She traced it slowly, a light caress that he suspected she didn't mean to turn him on, but it did. Part of it was her touch, another part the primal need to claim her as his own. To do everything he physically could to strengthen the bond between them.

"This part," she said, tracing the long scroll, "means fraternity. So it's the bond of brothers or brotherhood. Your family is from an ancient tribe so you all—all the tribes—have this mark to show each other they are brothers."

"I didn't realize we were part of an ancient tribe," Hemi said. But brotherhood resonated with him. He made bonds—strong bonds—wherever he was. He and his frat brothers from college were still close. His NASA brothers and sisters were close, as well.

"What else?"

"This mark signifies some sort of mysticism. My friend said he'd do further research owing to the fact that this could mean you had a shaman in your family or perhaps there was a vision involving your family," she said. "I think it means you have magic in your veins."

"You do?" he asked.

"Yes. When I met you and I looked at your face and saw this—" she touched his birthmark with light fingers "—I knew there was something powerful in you."

He was flattered by the way she watched him and honored him with her touch and her words. "You have that same power."

She shook her head.

But he stopped her. "Jessie, you have a strength that everyone envies. I have to be careful that I don't start relying on it."

She tipped her head to the side, watching him with her pretty, water-colored eyes, and he felt that catch in his chest again. That fear that he might not always be able to hold her like this.

She was his.

But he couldn't just say that. He had to woo her and make her want to be his. He suspected that if he walked away from NASA and the Cronus program, she'd follow him.

"What do you mean?"

"Just that quiet belief you have in everyone. I saw it when we were out in the wilderness. Velosi and Izzy both commented on it when we were back at the facility. How having you expect them to do well enabled them to be calmer about the decisions they were making. I bet you're awesome on the side of Everest or ice-trekking in the Arctic."

"Awesome? I guess. It's just that I know that panicking or stressing out never helps. I got that from my dad," she said.

"And the shark attack?" he asked.

She shrugged, and he noticed that her nipples were hard. He wanted to listen to what she was saying, her voice so sweet and melodic, not sad like it had been earlier, but he was transfixed by the streamlined grace of her body.

"Hemi?"

"Hmm...?"

"Your dick is poking out of the water, so I know you're not listening to me," she said.

He laughed. He heard the underlying current of desperation in it but he ignored that, pulling her closer and kissing her like they'd always have these moments together and he'd never have to let her go.

"My dick?"

"What word did you want me to use?" she asked.

"Uh, my hammer."

"That's right—Thor's hammer," she said with a saucy grin. He knew that nothing had been settled but in this moment, he knew they were on the same page. Both wanted to enjoy each other and celebrate the fact that they were safe and together.

JESSIE IGNORED THE BUTTERFLIES, or whatever the hell was in her stomach, and focused on Hemi. She wanted to ask him to stay. To give up going on the Cronus missions and become an instructor like she was. But then she remembered how she'd felt when Alexi hadn't wanted to do the television show with her.

How his not asking her to decline the offer had grown between them, ruining what they had. She had to ask him. Had to at least voice her concerns.

But as she looked into those big chocolate eyes of his, she let his laughter drive away the vestiges of fear and uncertainty. He appeared young and mischievous when he smiled at her like this. She couldn't ask him.

He tangled his hands in her hair and drew her forward on his lap. Their mouths met, tongues stroking each other, and she shifted until she felt him nudging at the entrance of her body.

She barely had to shift her hips and he slid into her. She sank all the way down on him but the water pushed her back up a bit. Hemi grabbed her hips and anchored her to him. He took his mouth from hers, and when he looked up at her, the laughter of a few moments ago was gone.

He was so dear to her. She hated to think of a time when she wouldn't be able to hold him like this.

She closed her eyes but there was no hiding from fear and the truth.

His mouth moved down her collarbone to her chest and then to her breast, taking her nipple into his mouth, sucking hard on it as he started to move inside her.

Her body caught fire and she put her hands on his shoulders, moving with him. Taking him. She wanted to memorize every moment of this night.

She squeezed for a moment, wondering if she could keep him here forever. Never let him go.

But then he shifted under her. His hands came up to her breasts and she threw her head back as need started burning inside of her. Her love mingled with the desire and she forgot about her fears for him and for their future.

She rode him like the wild god of thunder he was named after. Her space cowboy gave her a ride that she'd never forget, and when she felt her body start to tighten around him, as her climax edged closer, she glanced down and saw he was watching her.

She saw the emotions in his eyes and suddenly

she felt tears burning in hers. She didn't want to lose him. But she was afraid to keep him.

Her body clenched as her orgasm rolled through her and she fell forward, putting her head on his chest as he thrust up into her until he was spent.

He put his hands on her back and she tried to stop the tears that kept flowing down her cheeks. She lifted her hand to his chest so he'd think it was bathwater and not suspect she was crying.

She didn't want to let him forget it and there was no way she was going to let him leave her. Not the way Alexi had. Never.

Hemi had touched a part of her soul that no one else had. She'd searched her entire life for him without even realizing it. Now that she'd found him she had to make up her mind to keep him.

All this time she'd been afraid the man she loved would be taken from her while he was young.

The water had cooled around them, so Hemi stood up, lifting her, and they dried each other off. He looked tired, but Jessie was too restless to sleep.

In her mind were the words she wanted to say. The words that she realized she wouldn't utter. She couldn't take his dream from him. She'd heard how much he wanted to go into space.

"What is it? You look like you want to talk about something," Hemi said to her. He wrapped the towel around his trim hips, covering some of his tattoo.

"Do you want some hot chocolate?" she asked.

"I'd like that," he said, as they walked into the living area.

"I'll go make it. Why don't you find us a movie to watch?"

He nodded and reached for the remote, and she went into the kitchen. The control she had on her own emotions was shaky. She was acting like this was normal, but none of it was. She knew she loved Hemi. She knew that if he went on the Cronus mission she'd be a wreck the entire time he was away.

Love should feel different than this, she thought. But she honestly had no idea what love was. What she'd felt for Alexi paled in comparison to the volatile emotions that rollicked through her when she was with Hemi. He made everything so much…well, more.

All of her senses were tuned in to him. She was starting to be able to read him, to predict how he would act. He had become the other part of her soul and she wasn't sure that was a smart thing.

She got the milk from the fridge and poured it into a saucepan but didn't turn on the stove. Her mom had taught her to make hot chocolate on the yacht, when they'd been drifting out at sea chasing a bioluminescent species and there'd been nothing but water and sky surrounding them.

She was certain that feeling was what Hemi had when he went into space. She knew that he craved being out there the way her parents did being on the ocean. But her parents faced it with each other.

Not like this.

Not with one of them standing on the shore hoping the other made it back.

She put her hands on the counter, her head falling forward. She didn't know if she could do it. If she could love him and let him go.

"Jessie. Baby, what's the matter?"

She lifted her head to find him standing in the doorway, and she tried to speak but her throat closed up and all that came out was a sort of choked sound.

Hemi closed the distance between them, wrapped his arms around her and held her for a long time. Then he lifted her up and carried her back to bed. They didn't talk.

She knew they needed to discuss this but she didn't have the words, and it seemed he didn't, either. They slept in each other's arms, clinging as if they were afraid to let go.

HEMI HELD JESS close to him as the night deepened and then slowly gave way to dawn. They had cuddled each other, made love to each other, but they hadn't talked. In his heart he was afraid that even after he'd pursued her so vigorously, she wasn't going to stay with him.

A part of him felt like last night was her way of saying goodbye. He glanced at the glowing clock on the nightstand and saw that it was 4 a.m.

He turned on his side, knowing he needed distance to think.

She murmured in her sleep, and for a moment he wanted to stay. But if there was one thing he knew, it was that love couldn't be taken, it had to be given. It couldn't be forced. He'd seen that in his brother Manu's marriage. On paper Manu and Talia had been perfect. As a high-profile couple they'd looked like a match made in heaven. But Manu had admitted to Hemi that he'd married Talia because she fit the image of his ideal wife.

Hemi padded naked out of Jess's bedroom and

into the living room. He could see Venus through the window and remembered how excited he had been as a boy the first time he'd identified the planet and then showed it to his father. It had been the start of this journey to NASA.

He touched his tribal tattoo, looked down at it searching for answers. He knew Jessie had lost her lover. Had trained and hiked with him before they'd gone to climb Everest, and still he'd slipped through her fingers. He was very aware that his job was dangerous, as well. He didn't want to bring her more pain but he couldn't choose between her and his career.

And though he knew she'd never say the words, he sensed she wanted him to stay. He couldn't. He walked back through her house, grabbed his jeans from next to the bed and silently let himself out.

He walked at first, slowly, aware of the setting moon, watching him as it always did. But in the late-autumn morning he took no solace from the moon, but instead felt exposed and ashamed that he hadn't stayed to talk to her. That he hadn't been man enough to do what was needed.

He should tell her he loved her. Tell her that love was enough for them and that, yes, he would leave on his mission, but he'd come back to her.

But he didn't say any of that. Instead, he went to his quarters and realized that this place had never felt like home. It was only when he was with Jessie that he felt like he was home.

15

HE'D LEFT HER before she woke up. And she was angry. She wasn't sure what she had wanted to tell him, but she'd wanted to say something. She went for a run and then changed into her NASA Mick Tanner Training Facility golf shirt and a pair of khaki pants.

Checking her phone, she read an email from her mom. Her parents were in Fiji to restock the yacht and give a series of lectures at a local university. They invited her to visit.

She flagged the message and went to find Hemi.

The invite was nice, but right now her first priority was him. Last night had changed things between them. She'd stopped pretending that she didn't love him and she'd thought—really thought—that Hemi got that.

Then to wake up alone…

She stalked up the path and realized she was breathing heavily. She'd had her chance to ask him to stay with her, and she'd missed it. She realized a part of her was angry at herself and at the world.

She stopped.

What the hell was going on with her? She wasn't the type of woman to let a man upset her. He was an adult and his own person. He didn't have to wake her up before he left, her rational mind said.

But her gut said he'd snuck out to avoid talking to her. Maybe he'd sensed what she was holding back and was afraid she'd finally say it. She shivered a little in the early morning cold and wished she'd grabbed her fleece. She knew the weather was chilly. She just hadn't been thinking.

This was the kind of behavior that she had spent the last six weeks training the candidates to avoid. She was being emotional.

Well, a part of her felt like she was entitled, because she was in love with a stubborn man.

Hemi had admitted he was scared to die going on a mission and that should have given them something to talk about, but both of them had retreated behind their attraction.

But no longer. She wanted answers. What was he going to do next? Should she even recommend him for the mission? If she didn't, she'd just be keeping him here for herself and delaying the inevitable.

Hell, she knew she would recommend him. In fact, she'd already finished up her report on most of the candidates. There were several she wouldn't be recommending, based on their difficulties reacting to survival situations. The next training hurdle would be assembling the way station in the simulators, but Jessie wouldn't be part of that.

She had done her job. Had only a few more classes with this group and then she'd have a break before a new group of candidates arrived. Hemi would move on, as well, either as second-in-command for the first mission or as a regular crew member. Or he'd begin more intense preparation for the next phase.

He'd still be here training, but he wouldn't be her student any longer.

She'd shared her fear. Told him she didn't know what to do next and he'd…hell, he'd walked away without saying anything.

She'd let him push her and push her, and once she'd capitulated he backed away. From the very beginning she'd been the one running away from him, and now that she had stopped, wanted to put down roots and build a life with him, he'd vanished. Why?

She got to her office thinking of how she'd seduced Hemi here. She closed the door and put on her spare fleece, realizing that her hands were shaking. She needed answers. Or maybe a workout.

She had two hours until her next class, so she went to the locker room, changed and headed into the gym.

She heard the sound of the zero gravity treadmill and looked over at it.

Hemi.

He glanced up and saw her but didn't stop or take off his headphones. The anger she thought she'd managed to control sprang to life again.

Was this what he wanted? To just pretend that nothing had happened?

He was the one who had pursued her, made her really think about finding the one person she couldn't live without, and now he was jogging on that treadmill like she was…a stranger.

She turned away from him, went to the stationary bike, put her earbuds in and started cycling. She was very aware of Hemi on the other side of the room, though she kept her eyes carefully in front of her. But instead of concentrating on her cycling she could only feel the unanswered questions swirling inside her.

She was so busy trying to ignore Hemi that he startled her when he walked up next to her bike. He stood there with his hand extended and she slowed down, then reached up to remove her earbuds.

"Yes?"

"We need to talk," he said.

"You think?"

"What's up with you?"

"Nothing. Just didn't expect to wake up alone this morning," she said. "Glad to hear you think we should talk."

"You're angry," he said.

"Yup. So if you're not ready for this conversation then I suggest you leave."

"I'm ready," he said. "You want to do this here?"

"Not really," she said.

He turned on his heel and looked back at her to make sure she was following him to one of the private workout rooms. The room had an ice machine and a water cooler, as well as a padded table that was used by the facility's massage therapist.

Hemi locked the door behind them and turned to face her.

"I'm ready to discuss this," he said.

"Discuss what?" she asked. "Us? Last night you seemed like…well, like things had changed between us."

"They have. You know that. We both do," he said.

"I… You're right, but I don't want them to," she admitted.

"You have to face this, Jess. Or we will never be able to move on. It's going to be like you and Alexi all over again. And I'm afraid I'm not like Alexi. I can't just let it be. You know I can't."

She did know that.

"Say it," he commanded. "Say what's bothering you."

She took a deep breath. "I don't want you to go to space."

HEMI HADN'T WANTED to have this discussion with Jessie. He'd left early to avoid it. Last night had changed nothing. He was still confused about what he should do, and the fear that he'd always kept such a tight lid on was now making him question things he simply never had before.

He didn't want to talk to her, but he knew that they had to. A part of him wanted to just give in and say he'd stay here on the Bar T with her. They could train the other candidates and live together in that little cabin of hers.

But that wasn't his dream and he knew it.

He loved Jessie. Nothing had been clearer to him than his feelings for the tall, blonde warrior, but he also knew he couldn't give up the Cronus program.

All his life he'd wanted to be in this place, so why had he met Jessie now?

She was a complication that he hadn't anticipated and he wasn't sure how to handle it.

"I'm sorry I left without saying anything," he said.

She shook her head and gave him a hard look.

"What?" he asked.

"Don't lie to me," she said.

"I never have," he admitted. "I can't lie to you. I love you, Jessie. I think you've known it for a while. Lord knows I haven't really been trying to hide how I feel from you. I never expected someone like you to come into my life. Especially now. We're both very strong willed, we both know what we want and that makes me love you more, but it makes everything so much harder."

"Why? I'd think it would make it easier."

"Really?" he asked. "Don't you see that the more I love you, the more I want to keep you safe and happy?" Even at his own expense, he thought. He was tempted to do what he had to in order to keep her by his side. But then he remembered Manu. Love couldn't thrive when it was surrounded by lies. Or even half-truths that were told to make his partner happy.

Jessie was angry. He could tell from her stance and from her expression. Her eyes looked like they'd cut through him if they could.

"Okay. So if I asked you to never attempt Everest again, or go deep-sea diving, would you do it?" he asked. Because a part of him was sure she felt about her adventures the way he did about the Cronus missions.

She held her finger up. "Oh, no, you can't do that. This isn't about me and any treks or climbs I've been on or plan to do in the future—"

"Why wouldn't it be? That's the same thing as me going into space."

Her hand clenched into a fist and she bit her lower

lip before shaking her head slowly. "That's not fair. You know it's not the same. There is a chance I could survive a fall and there's absolutely zero likelihood of you surviving a fire on the launch pad. Zero, Hemi. You're not a god, despite your nickname, and if your rocket has a malfunction you will die."

"You're asking me to give up my dream…and live half a life. I told you how I feel about the stars, about being up there. How important this is to me," he said. He understood where she was coming from, but he wasn't going to walk away because of a failed trial run.

"This is precisely why I didn't want to say anything. It's an impossible choice, isn't it? I'm asking you to make a life with me and give us a chance."

"That's what I'm doing," he said. "Despite what I said earlier about Everest, I'd never ask you not to make another attempt at the summit, if that was what you wanted. Or if you wanted to go make a solo expedition to the Arctic, I'd support you. I'd be scared as hell the entire time, but I'd support you."

She wrapped her arms around her waist and looked up at him. Her icy-blue eyes were wide and revealed both fear and pain. He knew this wasn't an easy thing to discuss. But they both took risks all the time.

"We live our lives on the edge," he pointed out. "You were doing that long before you came to Texas and we fell in love, and I suspect you'll be doing it long after. It's a part of who you are and it's a part of who I am. I can't deny it any more than you can."

"I'm not asking you to—dammit, I didn't mean to ask you to deny any part of yourself. I just wanted… I just need… Maybe it would be better if I stopped thinking about what I need and focus on what you need," she said, at last. Her eyes were wet with tears that she didn't let fall and she dropped her arms.

"No. Don't. I need to know what you're thinking, Jess."

He took a step toward her but she shook her head and backed up, bumping into the massage table. "Jess—"

"Don't. Maybe you were right when you left. We're not ready to discuss this because I'm not sure what I want."

"Aside from me leaving the Cronus program?" he asked. That was his deal breaker. He loved her, and he had no idea if he could live without her, but he knew with downright certainty that life without NASA wasn't in the cards for him.

"No. Never. Like you said, it's part of who you are. I should never have said otherwise. I guess I'm going to have to figure out what I can live with."

"Can I help?" he asked.

She shrugged.

Before she could answer, someone knocked on the door. "Hello? Is someone in there?"

Jessie brushed past him to unlock the door. It was the massage therapist. "Sorry, I needed to talk to Thor about the way he was using the treadmill. The room is all yours now."

She walked away without looking back, and he felt something empty start to grow deep in his soul.

BY THE TIME Hemi got out of the locker room, Ace was calling all of them to a meeting. Some of the candidates in the main conference room were less chatty than others. The room was warm and got hotter as all twenty-four of the candidates filed in.

"Thanks for coming," Ace said. "Dennis wanted to be here but was called back to Houston. As you know, there has been a delay of three months in our first launch. Rocket development has run into a few snags. That being said, our timeline here is not being affected."

"What exactly were the snags?" Izzy asked. "I heard the rocket test failed."

"Testing of a new fuel combination failed," Ace said, "causing implosion after launch. I believe Dennis is going to hold a briefing once he has more information on exactly what went wrong. For now, I have to ask you all to have patience."

There were murmurs around the room but no one said anything else. Hemi leaned back against the wall, and Izzy, who stood next to him, looked up at him.

Ace seemed on edge and Hemi reckoned that was part and parcel of being in charge of the first mission. There were going to be setbacks. There always were. They all knew that. But an implosion…damned if that wasn't the one thing they all feared the most.

"Next up. We will be announcing the second-in-command for the first Cronus mission in ten days' time. Your instructors are putting the finishing touches on their recommendations. A few of you have work to make up in some of your classes and that will need to be finished by Friday. Also, there are three candidates who will need to do additional simulator exercises. They are Thor, Bombshell and

Velocity. Please see me after this meeting for your training times."

Ace lifted his gaze and made contact with everyone in the room. "Any questions?"

"Will the entire crew for the first mission be announced?" Velosi asked.

"No. Just the second-in-command. We will then go into Phase II training and the rest of the crew will be determined after that. I want you all to be aware that a private astronaut program is coming on board the Cronus Missions, as well, and they will be competing against you all for the remaining slots on the crew. I'm sure some of them will be familiar to you, while others are coming from European and Asian programs."

"Why are we teaming up with them?" Izzy asked.

"Money," Ace said. "Plus all of the governments with space programs have agreed that no one nation should have command of a way station. It needs to be cooperative, like the International Space Station," Ace said. "Any other questions?"

"When will Phase II start?" Velosi asked.

"Two weeks after we announce the second-in-command. Everyone will be given leave and encouraged to take a break so you can come back refreshed."

The meeting broke up after that and Hemi followed Izzy and Velosi down to Ace's office to find out more about the simulator training. The other two were chatting quietly, but half of Hemi's mind was still with Jessie. Where had she gone?

He pulled out his iPhone and sent her a text saying he didn't like the way they'd left things.

She sent him back the thumbs-up emoji.

Which didn't seem like a good response to him.

"You okay?" Velosi asked.

"Yeah, why?" Hemi asked.

"You just didn't seem to be paying attention."

"I'm distracted. Do you think they're rushing to get us up there?" Hemi asked.

"Maybe. It seems like everyone is on the knife's edge with this project. I hope three months gives them the time they need to fix the fuel issue," Izzy said.

"I'm sure it will. Sometimes it just takes a small tweak to fix things," Hemi said. He was confident they would solve the problem, but he wondered how many other setbacks they'd face before the mission was able to launch. "Why do you think Ace wants us doing more tests?"

"Isn't it clear?" Velosi said. "We must be the best."

Izzy punched him in the arm. "Watch out, Velocity, or that big head of yours won't fit in your helmet."

Hemi and Velosi laughed. Ace arrived a few minutes later, confirming their guess that they were in the running for second-in-command of the first mission. Hemi knew the next ten days were crucial. He spent the rest of the afternoon locked in a room with Ace, Izzy and Velosi. He concentrated and made notes on the briefing, knowing deep inside that, unless he screwed up, he could outperform Izzy and Velosi. He'd proven himself before.

He left the meeting and went to his quarters, checking his cell phone to see if Jessie had texted him again but she hadn't. He wanted to share the news with her. To share his excitement, but he wondered if she'd be happy for him.

He texted her again. Just a simple, I miss you. But there was no response, and he wondered if they'd said too much. Or maybe too little.

16

JESSIE AND HEMI were ignoring the fact that they hadn't dealt with their feelings about the rocket explosion—or each other.

She knew she needed a break and did the one thing she probably should have done the day she and Hemi had talked about everything—she asked for a few days of leave.

She packed her bikini and a change of clothes, and flew to Fiji to see her parents. As soon as she set foot on the *Calypso* she felt the tension she'd been carrying with her from Texas leave her body. Her mother was out and only her dad was on board. He came up from the galley wearing a pair of board shorts and no T-shirt. His chest was tanned from spending a lifetime in the sun, but he wore a hat on the top of his balding head to protect his face.

"Jessie, my girl," he said, opening his arms to her.

She dropped her bag and went to him, and he hugged her. It was the same big bear hug he'd given her countless times, and suddenly she realized how badly she'd needed it.

She hugged her dad back and just let the smell of his aftershave and the salty scent of the ocean soothe her troubled soul.

"Dad, it's so great to see you. What have you been up to?"

"My research has been…complicated," he said. "Why don't you go unpack in your cabin while I finish making us some lunch."

"Sounds great," she said, going down the stairs ahead of her dad and toward the smallish berth in the aft of the yacht that had always been hers. She stepped inside and sat down on the bunk. All she could think, as she looked around, was that Hemi would love the close quarters.

She rubbed the back of her neck.

This trip… She had no real agenda, just hope that maybe she'd be able to forget him. That her heart would find the distance reassuring and give her some insulation against the almost desperate love she felt for him.

But so far that wasn't happening. When she saw the water she wondered what it would be like if Hemi was here. She knew he'd grown up in California. She wondered if he had his scuba certification. Would he like to dive with her?

"Jess?" her dad called.

Just the sound of his voice made her feel safe. And she realized she needed that. She'd come to the one place where, even when she screwed up, she felt loved.

"Coming," she yelled back. She walked toward the galley and saw her dad had prepared shrimp and coconut curry and rice for lunch. She took the bowl he offered her, and a bottle of water, and climbed up to the deck again. She didn't have to wait for her dad to know he wanted to eat on the diving deck. He liked to sit there with his feet in the water.

She sat, and a moment later he joined her. Her dad was taller than she was by a few inches, and usually when people met them they said she resembled him. But her father had a quiet confidence that Jessie had never been sure she had.

"So, what's going on?" he asked.

She shook her head and looked out at the water in the harbor.

"Mom said there's a guy," he prompted her.

She smiled. "Yeah. His name is Hemi Barrett."

"I've heard of him," her father said.

"You have?"

"Yes. When you took the job at the Mick Tanner Training Facility, I did some research. He looks like he could have a long career with NASA."

"Yes. He will. He's a strong leader and he knows how to motivate the other candidates. He's the best I've seen in my classes."

"But that's not why you're here," her dad said.

"Nope." She put her lunch to one side, placed her hands behind her hips and leaned back on her forearms. "I like him, Dad. Really like him, and it makes no sense. He's not quiet like Alexi was. He's not anything like Alexi, except they both have a real core of inner strength."

"Alexi was one of a kind," her dad said. "What's the problem?"

She looked at him. But she couldn't find the words to tell him.

"Look, I know you're not afraid to admit your feelings. You already told your mom you really like him. Sounds to me like you love him. So what's the problem?"

She chewed her lower lip. "The rocket they'll be using is experimental, and during testing, it exploded. That's classified, Dad."

"Who am I going to tell?" he asked. "I'm sure that's just the beginning for the team developing the rocket. They'll get it fixed."

"Probably, but until that moment I hadn't thought about the fact that he could die. I was reassuring myself that I'd never be trying to hold on to him—" She broke off, because continuing was going to make her cry.

Dad put his bowl down and wrapped his arm around her shoulder, drawing her into his side.

"There are risks associated with everything, Jess."

"I know, Dad. But burning up on reentry… I'm not sure I can deal with that. And that's just one known risk. I have spent my entire life learning from you and Mom how to survive anything. I know techniques and skills that many other people don't have. I can find a way out of any situation, but not that one. I don't know how to help him survive something like that and I don't know how I'd survive if I let myself love him and…"

"Don't think about it," Dad said, squeezing her close. "Life is unexpected. You know that. Alexi was the best climber and the mountain got him. That's the way life is."

Her father, with his quiet voice, had gotten to the heart of it. She wanted to protect Hemi, to keep him safe, but she had forgotten that all the preparation and skills in the world weren't always enough.

ACE AND DENNIS had both noticed his distraction in the days since Jessie had left the facility, so Hemi wasn't really surprised when he was called into Ace's office.

"Ace, you wanted to see me?"

"Have a seat, Thor. Dennis will be here in a few minutes, but I asked you to come early so we could talk," Ace said, sitting back in his chair. Ace's office had a large picture of Mars taken by the Viking Orbiter, and around it were a few mission photos from Ace's different voyages into space. Sitting across from his friend, Hemi felt the weight of his distraction more keenly than he had before.

"Dennis is concerned about you being chosen as my second-in-command," Ace said. "Frankly, I am, too. What's going on with you lately?"

"Sorry. I…it's Jessie. The rocket explosion freaked her out and things are kind of shit between us right now."

"How did she hear about the explosion?" Ace asked.

"Molly."

"Dammit. I'm sorry. Molly and I have been going round and round on this, too. She thinks I should step down and lead from the ground. I can't do that," Ace said.

"I know. That's pretty much where I am with Jessie. And if I go, I'm not sure she'll be waiting for me the way Molly will be for you," Hemi said. "Women."

"Can't live with them," Dennis said as he stepped into the room. "Life's not as nice without them."

"Sir," Hemi said, standing up. "Took the words right out of my mouth."

"So your problem is a female one?" Dennis asked, walking in and taking the seat next to Hemi.

Hemi sat back down and stretched his legs out in front of him, trying to seem cool, but he was tense. Not just because his future with NASA was on the line but also because he still wasn't sure what he was going to do about Jessie.

"Yes," Hemi said. "I know I've let it affect some of my training, and I'm sorry about that."

"Can you get it under control?" Dennis asked. "I'm going to level with you, Thor. You're still out-performing everyone else in your group, but we can tell you're not yourself. Do you need some time off to figure this out? Fix whatever is going on in your personal life and then come back fresh?"

Hemi would have loved that, except that Jessie was gone. He had no idea where. They'd never gotten a weekend away together and now he was being offered time, but she wasn't here.

"I'd love it, but my woman isn't here so it wouldn't do me any good."

"Jessie?" Dennis asked.

"Yeah," Hemi said. "Is that a problem?"

"Not at all. She asked for leave and you've been… well, not present, so I was just putting it together," Dennis said.

"We had an idea that we'd like to run by you," Ace said.

"Sure," he said. Nice to know that he'd been fooling everyone. Not.

"We'd like you to go with Izzy and Velosi to tour some schools in California. You'll talk to elementary school kids. Sound good?"

"Sure. Why California?"

"We had a request from the school system near Pasadena, and we were going to be sending you in that direction, anyway. The Jet Propulsion Laboratory wants to do some tests with weight to check out the rocket simulator. When you're done at the schools, the rest of the Cronus candidates will meet you at JPL," Ace said.

"Okay. When do we leave?" Hemi asked. He wasn't sure when Jessie was getting back, and to be honest, maybe getting away was what he needed. He could focus on being an astronaut and stop trying to figure out how to get her to admit that his dying scared her.

"If you'd like take some extra time to see your folks," Dennis said, "you can leave on Friday. We are sending Izzy and Velosi on Sunday, since your first school appointment is Monday."

Going home and seeing his folks…sounded great. He needed to be around people who loved him unconditionally, so he could figure out what he was going to do next. He loved Jessie, but there was no denying that she pushed him in ways he wasn't too sure that he liked. And he definitely didn't want to lose the advantage he'd created for himself through hard work on the Cronus program.

"I'd appreciate that," Hemi said. "My mom will be very happy to have me home for the weekend."

"No doubt. Molly and I are flying out Friday, too," Ace said. "I promised her some time away from the facility… Something romantic."

"Good luck with that. I never could find a woman who understood how demanding this job was," Dennis said.

"Molly gets it. She just needs…well, reassurance that I'm not going flake on her."

Dennis nodded to both men as he stood up. "Glad that's sorted. I'm going to Houston while you all are in California, but I'll be back here to oversee the classes. We've got a Senate committee that wants a tour and I'm going to push for more funding. I want to get a second underwater simulator installed."

"Good luck," Ace said.

Dennis left the room and Hemi turned toward his friend. "I'm sorry I've been so distracted."

"I get it," Ace said. "Falling for a woman…it's not easy and it takes work to get it right."

How much work? Hemi wondered. He wasn't afraid to keep working to make things with Jessie more permanent, but did she want that? It would be nice to have a few days away from here. Maybe it would give him a better perspective on what to do next.

By Saturday, Jessie was starting to feel more herself again. Her parents had let her have some space and had also taken her diving, which had slowly given her the time she needed to think.

She missed Hemi and knew leaving the way she had couldn't have been easy on him. Finally, after days of avoiding it, she sent him a text message.

It's me. I'm sorry for the way I left.

She saw the notification that her message had been delivered and a few moments later that it had been read.

She waited, looking anxiously at those three little dots on her phone that indicated Hemi was typing a response.

Glad to hear it. Are you coming back?

She texted back, Yes. I'd hoped Ace would tell you I took a week off to visit my parents.

You could have told me yourself.

I know. Are you still mad?

Yes. I get why you left. I needed to get away, too. But it was the way you did it. I wish you'd said something. We never had a chance to fix things.

I know. I'm sorry.

There was no immediate response and she kept hitting the refresh button, hoping that it was just a slow connection.

A moment later the video chat app started ringing. She saw Hemi's name and number, and glanced in the mirror to check her appearance.

Her hair had dried but it was flat, and her face was a little bit sunburned. She answered the call but turned the camera so it faced the ceiling in her room.

"Jessie?"

"I'm here but I look like I've been diving all day."

"I don't mind," he said. "I've spent the day fishing."

She picked up her phone. Hemi looked tired but so damned good to her. She'd missed him more than she'd realized. She reached a finger out to touch the screen and noticed that he was doing the same to her.

"What are we going to do?" she asked. There was no escaping the way she felt about him. Now what she needed to figure out was if she was strong enough to love him.

To let that love into every corner of her body and soul.

Honestly, she had no idea how she was going to keep it out.

"Where are you?" she asked.

"In California. NASA sent me out here to do some elementary school visits, and then we have meetings at JPL at the end of the week."

"The kids are going to love you," she said.

"I usually do okay with little ones. They love to ask questions about silly things that we do in space."

"I bet," she said, aware that she was making small talk instead of saying what she really wanted to. "Where are you staying?"

"In a hotel near the lab. If you had still been in Texas…"

"But I'm not. I'm with my parents, too. What does it say about me that I went home?"

He shrugged.

"I just needed some distance. Hemi, you overwhelm me and sometimes it's too much," she said at last. She watched his face, saw him look over his shoulder and then move until he was outside. He looked down at the screen again, and in that moment she knew that she had a lot of power over Hemi. She had hurt him without meaning to. He had made sure he was alone to speak to her.

She and Alexi had both been introverted, so she could spend time by herself sorting issues out while he did his own thing. Hemi was different. She'd known that from the beginning, but only now was it truly making sense.

"I guess that's why I retreat into myself when I want to figure things out," she said.

"Probably. Listen, we need to get this settled between us. I was distracted at the training center. I know it's not your fault," he said. "I'm not blaming you, but I can't pretend you mean nothing to me. That the unsettled nature of this relationship doesn't get to me."

She sighed. The last thing she wanted was to distract him from his training. The last few days with her parents and all that time alone in the sea had given her a chance to think. Hemi needed his career the same way she needed hers.

He was doing something few others were capable of, and seeing him now, she knew she had to stop thinking about the hurt that might come if something happened to him. She had to focus instead on making the most of the time they had together.

"I agree."

"Good. I don't want to do this on the phone," he said. "I get back to Houston on Saturday. When are you coming back?"

"Saturday afternoon. Probably with a lot of jet lag."

"Would you meet me at the Houston Hilton on Saturday night? We can have dinner and talk. See what we want to do next," he asked.

She nodded. "Yes, that sounds like a good idea."

"Great. I know a really nice restaurant where we can go. Bring something dressy."

"How dressy?"

"Well, I liked that gray silk dress you wore the night we met," he said.

"You did?"

"Yes. I couldn't take my eyes off you."

"You looked pretty good to me, too. I was standing there trying to be invisible and you wouldn't let me. Just walked up to me and made me feel…"

"What?" he asked.

"Like I was the only woman in the room," she said, and hung up because she didn't want to say any more.

_17_

HEMI FLEW BACK to Houston early with his brother Manu. A little bit of jet lag dogged him, but he wanted time to get everything set up for Jessie. He knew it for sure now: he needed Jessie in his life.

She completed him. It would sound trite if he said it out loud, but it resonated deep in his soul.

"I've never seen you this nervous," Manu said.

"I don't think I've ever wanted something to be perfect before."

"Kaikaina," Manu said, using the phrase that meant "younger brother" in Hawaiian. "Life isn't perfect, but that doesn't mean that it isn't exactly what it should be."

Hemi clapped his brother on the shoulder and scanned the main room of the executive suite he'd rented for the night. Manu had helped him get the room exactly how he wanted it. Spending time apart had just made Hemi more determined to have Jessie in his life _and_ continue his career with the Cronus program.

Now if he could just convince Jessie of that. He

had the new rocket specs and the report that JPL had generated on the initial test failure and how they'd corrected it.

He put the report on the coffee table where he'd also placed a traditional wishing bowl, which he'd ordered online. He heard that it was the kind they used in the South Pacific islands where Jessie had grown up.

He had a tiny slip of paper where he'd written his deepest wish and he wanted her to add hers to the bowl.

"What time is she supposed to be here?" Manu asked.

"Seven," Hemi said, glancing at his watch. Dammit, it was only three in the afternoon. "That's hours away."

"Good. You need to relax or you're going to blow it," Manu said.

"Telling me to relax isn't helping," Hemi said.

Manu chuckled, and Hemi felt a little like he had when they'd been kids and he wanted to punch his brother for making fun of him.

"I know. Remember when I played in my first national championship and I was bouncing around and Dad kept saying 'be calm'?"

Hemi smiled at the memory. Manu had looked like he was going to put his fist into the wall if their father had offered that advice one more time. Manu had been a linebacker but was retired now and was a coach for special teams—the guys who went on during specific plays. All of the Barrett men were built large and muscly.

"Yeah, I do. So I guess you know to stop saying it to me," Hemi said.

"Maybe. But what you don't know is when I walked out of the locker room to get away from Dad's well-meaning advice I saw Mom. She was standing there with a few of the wives and other mothers and she came over to me…"

Manu walked over to Hemi and took his forearms in his grip. "She told me that the outcome was already written. That my nerves weren't going to do anything but change my journey, not the outcome. And, little brother, I think you know this."

Hemi looked into Manu's eyes. They weren't the dark brown that he and his other two brothers had; they were a blend of green, brown and blue like their mother's. Hemi had always thought they were shamans' eyes.

"I'm afraid to trust what I hope will be the outcome," Hemi admitted.

"Accept it. Do you love her?"

"I do, Manu. Way more than I ever thought I could love a woman," Hemi admitted.

"You've never loved lightly," Manu reminded him. "I'd find it hard to believe you would do so now."

He nodded. His brother was right.

"Come on. Let's go shoot some pool for a few hours so you can take your mind off her."

Hemi followed his brother out of the hotel and down the street to a pool hall that he'd visited before with Ace and some of the other astronauts. Manu was recognized as "the enemy" by a few Houston football fans, and he endured some good-natured ribbing about both wins and losses he'd brought to Houston.

They played pool and drank orange soda—Manu's favorite—and slowly Hemi let the wisdom of his brother and his parents sink into him. He and Jessie had been drawn to each other from the beginning.

It hadn't been the right time for either of them to find someone to start a relationship with but it had happened anyway.

She'd tried to make him into her lover, and only her lover, but they enjoyed a close connection. He knew that her fears about the space program were warranted. He understood that if she were to start planning another of her expeditions he'd fear for her the same way. But he also felt something that couldn't be denied.

Something that had been there all along.

Love.

It wasn't the kind that was just for now or would disappear after the rush of passion cooled—if that ever happened between them, and he doubted it would—he knew he'd still love her.

She wasn't just the other half of his soul, she was part of him now. The certainty of that enabled him to finally start to relax.

He put his hand into his pocket to touch the ring that he'd brought with him from California. Tonight he would ask Jessie to marry him. Tonight he would show her that together they were stronger than they could ever be apart.

Manu glanced up from signing an autograph and gave him a long look before smiling and winking at him.

"Figured it out, little brother?"

"Damned straight," Hemi said. They went back to the

hotel and Manu left to go to his suite. Hemi showered and changed and as he waited to meet Jessie a little bit of the nervousness crept back in.

"JESSIE! OVER HERE."

Jessie scanned the crowd at Houston International Airport and found Rina standing near the exit, waving at her. Everyone was meeting relatives and friends, and the airport was decorated for the holidays.

Jessie stared at the Christmas decorations as she hurried through the throngs of people to Rina's side. The strawberry blonde wore a pair of jeans and a leather jacket, and had a pair of sunglasses holding her hair back like a headband.

Jessie was glad to see a familiar face after hours on a plane. She pulled her suitcase along behind her as she walked over to Rina.

"Hey. I wasn't expecting anyone to pick me up," Jessie said, giving Rina a one-armed hug.

"I figured. But when Molly said you were coming in I decided you might like some company. Was I wrong?" Rina asked.

"No, you weren't," Jessie admitted. She was tired of her own company. The days diving and being with her parents had made one thing clear. She wasn't ready to walk away from Hemi. But figuring out how to live with the fear he'd awakened in her was hard.

She was no closer to the answer now than she had been when she left.

No, that wasn't true. At least now she knew that her heart wasn't going to be easily turned from him. Hemi was there now. He was in her heart and she needed to figure out if living with him, with the fear of what could happen, was possible for her.

"I'm glad. So, where to?"

"Do you know I'm meeting Hemi here?" Jessie asked.

"Yes. I thought you might like some girl time. You know, mani-pedis or even just some wine and conversation," Rina said. "If I'm wrong I'll leave."

Jessie shifted her carry-on from one shoulder to the other. "I could use some girl time before I meet Hemi tonight. My parents are great, but they are my parents."

Rina laughed and reached for Jessie's suitcase. "Let me get this. Just in case you felt that way, I booked us into a spa for some treatments."

"Sounds great." Like an adventure for her new life.

Jessie laughed and talked—but not about Hemi, which underscored how much she'd been thinking and worrying over the last few days. Rina caught her up on all the ranch gossip and even on what was going on with their favorite basketball team, the Mavericks. Then, after all their spa treatments, they went shopping and Jessie bought a new dress for her dinner with Hemi.

She wanted to be the woman he couldn't take his eyes off again. She wanted him to be so enchanted by her that he would never let her go.

Rina dropped her off at the Hilton just before seven, waving goodbye and wishing her luck. Jessie had never felt so scared in her entire life. The irony wasn't lost on her. She'd rather face a blizzard on Everest than walk into that hotel and see something in Hemi's eyes that would tell her it was over.

When she walked into the lobby, she saw the broad shoulders of a man who looked like Hemi. But when she got closer, he turned and she could see that this wasn't her man—but they shared a resemblance.

"Hello, Jessie. I'm Manu, Hemi's brother," he said, holding out his hand to her.

She took it and he lifted it to his mouth, kissing the back of it. "My brother's description of you was spot-on. You are more gorgeous than all the stars in the sky."

She smiled at that. There was no lack of charm in the Barrett gene pool. "Where is Hemi?"

"He's asked me to meet you and escort you to his suite."

"His suite? I thought we were having dinner," she said.

"You are. He…he has something special planned for you. Is that okay?" Manu asked. "Or do you need to be in public?"

"No, I don't. I trust your brother," she said.

"Good. If you didn't then you're not the right woman for him," Manu said. "This is none of my business, but my brother…"

Her heart melted as she realized that Manu was trying to warn her not to hurt Hemi. That reassured her that what he felt for her was genuine.

"I love him," she said. "I'm just not sure that is enough to make this work."

"Fair. As I said, it's not really any of my business. But he's my little brother and I don't want to see him hurt."

"We're definitely on the same page there," she

said. Hemi was lucky to have siblings, even though he'd said they were a pain. "Am I overdressed?"

"You're just right," Manu said. He led the way to the elevator and used his concierge-level key to access the floor where Hemi's suite was. He led the way down the hall, keeping up small talk but she wasn't really listening. Her heart beat so loudly that she almost turned and bolted for the emergency stairs. She thought she wouldn't stop running until…until what? If she left now she'd never have Hemi in her life.

She'd spend the rest of it watching him from afar and still loving him and missing him.

Manu stopped in front of the door and handed her the key.

"Have a good evening," he said before walking away.

She hesitated, then raised her hand and knocked.

"Come in," Hemi called.

She opened the door and walked into the candlelit room. He'd scattered rose petals on the ground, and she stopped and took off the high-heeled sandals she wore. She put her purse on the table by the door and walked slowly down the rose path toward Hemi, who stood in the middle of the room.

There were lights all around him and he looked like he was standing in the middle of the cosmos. She wasn't sure how he'd done it but she felt as though she was floating.

He reached his hand out to her and she took a step forward. Their fingers brushed and something electric passed between them.

"Jessie."

SHE WORE A cranberry satin dress that hugged her curves and ended just above the knee. Her hair was up with only a few strands framing her face, similar to the style she'd worn on the night they met. He'd dressed in the same tuxedo he'd worn that night. Her eyes… They sparkled as she took in the room but her focus never really left him.

He had so many things he wanted to say. Words he'd practiced over and over again in his head escaped him now that he was looking at her.

All he'd been able to muster was her name. When she'd taken his hand, it had been all he could do not to draw her close, wrap himself around her and never let her go.

He knew he was never going to be the same after this night.

That was as it should be.

A man should only propose to a woman who changed him fundamentally, made him realize that life was better with a partner than lived solo.

"Hemi. You look so sexy in a tux," she said.

Then she dropped his hand and closed the distance between them. Wrapped her arms around him and buried her face in his neck. Her breath was hot against his skin, and when she spoke he had to strain to hear her.

"I missed you so damned much," she said, a catch in her voice. She stepped back and wiped at a tear in the corner of her eye.

"I'm sorry for the way I left. I needed time to think and I didn't know if I could do that with you so close to me," she admitted.

"It's okay. I abandoned you first. I should have

stayed that morning and talked to you like an adult, but I was afraid. For the first time, Jessie, I was afraid of my job. We never talk about fire at NASA, not really. We have fire safety protocols and everything on any of our spacecraft is fire retardant. But then, all of a sudden, there it was. In my face and more real than I wanted it to be," he said. "I was trying to figure my own way around it and didn't know how to deal with your fear…"

He took a step closer to her. She smelled of summertime and flowers, and he closed his eyes. "I was afraid that if you had asked me to quit, I would have. And I know that it would have been a promise I can't keep."

She put her fingers to her mouth and shook her head. He didn't like that she was taking so much of this on herself. It was his fear that had driven him away from her, and it was love that was bringing them back together.

His parents had always said that love was the strongest power in the world and for the first time he actually got it. He got how much braver he felt knowing that Jessie was back in his life and by his side.

"I would have asked. I wanted so badly to get rid of the fear that was gnawing through my soul at the thought of you trapped in a rocket like that. But now…after having been away from you for so long, I know I can't. I can't ask you to give up your dream and I can't walk away from you," she said.

"I wouldn't ask you to walk away. If you tried, I think I would follow you," he said. "Our lives are meant to be together. I need you in ways I never thought I'd need anyone."

"Me, too," she admitted. "I thought about what you said and about how I wouldn't back down from an expedition just because there was danger involved. That wasn't fair of me to think you should."

"It was fair. Love makes us want to keep each other safe and I do get that," he said.

"But you can't give up who you are. Any more than I can. I accept that, Hemi. Just as I've come to understand that the love I have for you will not be denied. Nothing could make me feel safer than being by your side."

"Jessie—"

"No, let me do this," she said, rubbing her hands down her sides and then taking a step closer to him and going down on one knee. "I know, I'm not perfect, but—"

He dropped to his knee in front of her and put his finger over her lips. "Don't you dare do that. I love you too much to let you ever say you're not perfect. You are the only woman for me. The only one I want."

"It's the same for me," she admitted. "I was planning to ask you to marry me."

"Well, too bad," he said.

"What do you mean, too bad?" she said.

"I'm asking," he insisted, pulling the ring out of his pocket and holding it up. "It was my grandmother's ring."

He looked down at the simple band of gold that was set with aquamarines. It reminded him of both Jessie's eyes and the oceans as they looked when he observed them from space.

"I will marry you," Hemi said, and then he winked at her. "Will you marry me?"

"Yes!"

He put the ring on her finger and then put his hands on her face, tracing her cheekbones before leaning in to kiss her. The kiss was long and deep, and Hemi tried to tell her with his kiss that he'd never leave her even when he was away on a mission and he'd always love her.

"Did they make the announcement on who is going to be second-in-command on the first mission?" she asked.

He shook his head. "It's going to be on Monday."

"So, do we have this weekend here or are you needed back at the facility?"

"I'm all yours," he said.

"Exactly what I wanted to hear."

18

JESSIE STOOD IN the corner as the party raged on at the training facility on the Bar T. The big, open conference room was decked out for the event. She had had enough of partying and celebrating, but that was part of her life now. Hemi had been named the second-in-command for the inaugural Cronus mission. He would be part of the team assembling the way station parts remotely from the shuttle before the team was deployed onto the station.

"Still don't like parties much?" Hemi asked, coming up on her left and putting his hand in the middle of her back. Her dress was one of those deceptively demure ones with long sleeves and a boatneck but a plunging back. Hemi hadn't been able to keep his hands off her all night.

"Not really," she admitted. "I'd rather be alone with my own astronaut."

He arched one eyebrow at her. "Your own?"

"You know that you belong to me, Hemi 'Thor' Barrett," she said, placing one hand on his chest and then reaching around behind him and grabbing his butt to pull him close to her.

He laughed and it made her smile. It was full of joy, and sent a familiar wave of heat through her body.

"Yeah. Well, you belong to me, too," he said, pulling her closer and lowered his head. "And as soon as we leave here tonight I'm going to make you mine. Leave my mark on you inside and out."

"I can't wait," she said, rubbing a hand over his jaw, where the usual stubble had become a close-cropped beard. He'd been letting it grow out and she liked the way the soft hair felt against her fingers. His eyes were sensual as he watched her.

The band started playing something slow and jazzy, and she realized it was the song she'd requested. "Shoot the Moon," a cover of the Norah Jones song. She took Hemi's hand in hers and led him toward the dance floor.

"I asked for this song."

"Good," he said, pulling her into his arms and swaying gently with her around the floor. "This song is on the playlist you made for me."

"It is," she admitted. Realizing he was going to be leaving on the mission had made her very aware that she wanted to be with him. The astronauts could take a few personal effects with them. The playlists she'd been developing. The collage she was making, a blend of patterns that she'd found in doing more research on Hemi's tattoo and the photos she'd compiled of their time together. She was trying to surround him with their life so he'd have it with him forever.

He swayed, singing under his breath as they moved around the dance floor and her heart felt too full. She stopped dancing and squeezed him to her. Hugged him so close that she thought she'd absorb him into her very being.

"I love you," she said.

He looked down at her. "I love you, too, Jessie. More than I thought possible."

The song ended and he took her hand, leading her out of the party. The path to their cottage was well lit and they'd walked it many times. The winter moon was full and bright over them and Hemi shrugged out of his tux jacket, giving it to her to wear as they held hands and walked.

"All my life I've never had a home, not a place where I could put stuff or that I longed to get back to," she said. "But you've given me one here in Texas. And I know that no matter what the future holds, this place will always be that for me."

"Why Texas?"

"Because it's where I fell in love with you," she said.

He lifted her into his arms and carried her the rest of the way to the cabin. He made love to her with all the passion she'd come to anticipate from him, and afterward, as they lay in each other's arms, she knew that her love for Hemi was growing stronger with each day.

"You complete me, Jessie. Thanks to you I know

I'm a better man and a stronger leader. I can't imagine my life without you by my side."

"Me, too," she said. "You've given me the moon and the stars."

* * * * *

*Prepare for blastoff with BEYOND THE LIMITS,
the next story in Katherine Garbera's exciting
SPACE COWBOYS miniseries!
In stores May 2017.*

REQUEST YOUR FREE BOOKS!
2 FREE NOVELS PLUS 2 FREE GIFTS!

H HARLEQUIN®

Blaze®

red-hot reads!

YES! Please send me 2 FREE Harlequin® Blaze® novels and my 2 FREE gifts (gifts are worth about $10). After receiving them, if I don't wish to receive any more books, I can return the shipping statement marked "cancel." If I don't cancel, I will receive 4 brand-new novels every month and be billed just $4.74 per book in the U.S. or $5.21 per book in Canada. That's a savings of at least 14% off the cover price. It's quite a bargain. Shipping and handling is just 50¢ per book in the U.S. and 75¢ per book in Canada.* I understand that accepting the 2 free books and gifts places me under no obligation to buy anything. I can always return a shipment and cancel at any time. Even if I never buy another book, the two free books and gifts are mine to keep forever.

150/350 HDN GH2D

Name _____ (PLEASE PRINT)

Address _____ Apt. #

City _____ State/Prov. _____ Zip/Postal Code

Signature (if under 18, a parent or guardian must sign)

Mail to the **Reader Service:**
IN U.S.A.: P.O. Box 1867, Buffalo, NY 14240-1867
IN CANADA: P.O. Box 609, Fort Erie, Ontario L2A 5X3

Want to try two free books from another line?
Call 1-800-873-8635 or visit www.ReaderService.com.

* Terms and prices subject to change without notice. Prices do not include applicable taxes. Sales tax applicable in N.Y. Canadian residents will be charged applicable taxes. Offer not valid in Quebec. This offer is limited to one order per household. Not valid for current subscribers to Harlequin Blaze books. All orders subject to credit approval. Credit or debit balances in a customer's account(s) may be offset by any other outstanding balance owed by or to the customer. Please allow 4 to 6 weeks for delivery. Offer available while quantities last.

Your Privacy—The Reader Service is committed to protecting your privacy. Our Privacy Policy is available online at www.ReaderService.com or upon request from the Reader Service.

We make a portion of our mailing list available to reputable third parties that offer products we believe may interest you. If you prefer that we not exchange your name with third parties, or if you wish to clarify or modify your communication preferences, please visit us at www.ReaderService.com/consumerchoice or write to us at Reader Service Preference Service, P.O. Box 9062, Buffalo, NY 14240-9062. Include your complete name and address.

HB15

*Regan Macintosh doesn't trust Jamie Quinn's roguish
charm, but her resolve to keep the sexy stranger away is
starting to wane…and if she's not careful, their hungry
passion could make them both lose control.*

Read on for a sneak preview of
THE MIGHTY QUINNS: JAMIE,
the latest book in Kate Hoffmann's beloved series
THE MIGHTY QUINNS.

Regan walked out into the chilly night air. A shiver
skittered down her spine, but she wasn't sure it was
because of the cold or due to being in such close proximity
to Jamie. Her footsteps echoed softly on the wood deck,
and when she reached the railing, Regan spread her hands
out on the rough wood and sighed.

She heard the door open behind her and she held her
breath, counting his steps as he approached. She shivered
again, but this time her teeth chattered.

A moment later she felt the warmth of his jacket
surrounding her. He'd pulled his jacket open and he stood
behind her, his arms wrapped around her chest, her back
pressed against his warm body.

"Better?"

It was better. But it was also more frightening. And
more exhilarating. And more confusing. And yet it seemed
perfectly natural. "I should probably get to bed," Regan
said. "I can't afford to fall asleep at work tomorrow."

He slowly turned her around in his arms until she faced him. His lips were dangerously close to hers, so close she could feel the warmth of his breath on her cheek.

"I know you still don't trust me, but you're attracted to me. I'm attracted to you, too. I want to kiss you," he whispered. "Why don't we just see where this goes?"

"I think that might be a mistake," she replied.

"Then I guess we'll leave it for another time," he said. "Good night, Regan." With that he turned and walked off the deck.

Her heart slammed in her chest and she realized how close she'd come to surrender. He was right; she was attracted to him. She had wanted to kiss him. She'd been thinking about it all night. But in the end common sense won out.

Regan slowly smiled. She was strong enough. She *could* control her emotions when he touched her. Though he still was dangerous, he was just an ordinary guy. And if she could call the shots, maybe she could let something happen between them.

Maybe he'd ask to kiss her again tomorrow. Maybe then she'd say yes.

Don't miss
THE MIGHTY QUINNS: JAMIE
by Kate Hoffmann, available in February 2017
wherever Harlequin® Blaze® books and ebooks are sold.

www.Harlequin.com

HBEXP0117

Turn your love of reading into
rewards you'll love with
Harlequin My Rewards

**Join for FREE today at
www.HarlequinMyRewards.com**

Earn **FREE BOOKS** of your choice.

Experience **EXCLUSIVE OFFERS** and contests.

Enjoy **BOOK RECOMMENDATIONS**
selected just for you.

PLUS! Sign up now
and get **500** points
right away!

Earn
FREE
REWARDS
Join
Today!
HarlequinMyRewards.com

HARLEQUIN®

A *Romance* FOR EVERY MOOD™

JUST CAN'T GET ENOUGH?

Join our social communities
and talk to us online.

You will have access to the latest
news on upcoming titles and special
promotions, but most importantly,
you can talk to other fans about your
favorite Harlequin reads.

Harlequin.com/Community

 Facebook.com/HarlequinBooks

 Twitter.com/HarlequinBooks

Pinterest.com/HarlequinBooks

HARLEQUIN®

A *Romance* FOR EVERY MOOD™

Stay up-to-date on all your
romance-reading news with the
Harlequin Shopping Guide,
featuring bestselling authors, exciting new
miniseries, books to watch and more!

The newest issue will be delivered right to you
with our compliments! There are 4 each year.

Signing up is easy.

EMAIL

ShoppingGuide@Harlequin.ca

WRITE TO US

HARLEQUIN BOOKS
Attention: Customer Service Department
P.O. Box 9057, Buffalo, NY 14269-9057

OR PHONE

1-800-873-8635 in the United States
1-888-343-9777 in Canada

Please allow 4-6 weeks for delivery of the first issue by mail.